The Record Player

and

Other Stories

The Record Player

and

Other Stories

Winifred Moranville

Minnesota Voices Project
Number 94
New Rivers Press 2000

First edition
Library of Congress Card Catalog Number: 98-89719
ISBN: 0-89823-198-1

Cover illustration and design by John Keely
Interior design and typesetting by Patrie Design

Printed in Canada

This is a work of fiction. The names, characters, and events described in
these stories are the author's creation.

New Rivers Press is a nonprofit publishing house with a commitment to
literature by emerging writers.

The publication of *The Record Player and Other Stories* has been made
possible by generous grants from the Jerome Foundation and Dayton's,
Mervyn's California, and Target stores by the Dayton Hudson Foundation.

This activity is made possible in part by a grant provided by the Minnesota
State Arts Board, through an appropriation by the Minnesota State
Legislature. In addition, this activity is supported in part by a grant from
the National Endowment for the Arts.

Additional support has been provided by the General Mills Foundation,
the McKnight Foundation, the Star Tribune Foundation, and the
contributing members of New Rivers Press.

NATIONAL
ENDOWMENT
FOR THE
ARTS

MINNESOTA
STATE ARTS BOARD

New Rivers Press
420 North Fifth Street
Minneapolis, MN 55401

www.newriverspress.org

For David Wolf

Grateful acknowledgment is made to the publications
in which some of these stories previously appeared:

Iowa Woman: "Fred's Beer"

Missouri Review: "Dressing It Up"

Pleiades: A Journal of New Writing:
"The Health Food Junkie Juice and Sandwich Bar"

Roanoke Review: "Monsieur Pherlon"

Sketch: "The Record Player"

CONTENTS

The Record Player

and

Other Stories

BARN SHADOW DANCE

In summer and early fall, before the harvest, the corncrib was our spaceship. By then, most rooms had been swept clean of the corn and feed for the hogs, cows, and horses, who paid no attention to our great spaceship's ascent. The older cousins commanded from the cupola; the rest manned our positions in the rooms, nooks, and on the platforms and machinery at ground level. As one of the oldest boys in the family, I had plenty of turns as commander of our great vessel.

Now, years have passed and I'm flying above the farm in the company jet. My colleagues and I have just finished a meeting in Omaha; the jet is on its way back to the firm in Chicago. The pilot has agreed to drop me off at the Humboldt County airport today, the day before our grandmother's funeral. We are making our descent.

"Look," I say. "There. That's where I grew up." I point out the specks of white, a few dots of red and black spread across the acres: three farmhouses, a barn, a corncrib, and a sprinkling of sheds, chicken coops, pig pens. From above, they stand out against the fields of drying corn. Up here, the contrast is sharp.

But I know that the paint on the buildings has faded and boards are missing. The buildings themselves are empty and silent. I know that the quiet will be the first thing each of us— all the cousins who once manned the spaceship—will notice as we pull in from elsewhere for the funeral.

At the visitation, there are many, many bouquets of flowers, which is surprising, as our grandmother often complained that everyone she knew in her youth had been dead twenty years. She would have been a hundred and two the next month.

There are flowers from the family and our friends, of course, but many bouquets have been sent from companies where we, her grandchildren, are employed. We can't help it, and mostly it's for fun, but we start to compare the flowers sent by the firms.

"Look," Margaret, the teacher, says. "Here's why health insurance premiums are so high." She points to an elaborate standing spray of roses, carnations, lilies—an arrangement larger than any—sent by an insurance company.

"Maybe that will be my next career change—insurance," I say.

"Hey, I'm not the one who flew into town on the company jet," my cousin the insurance executive says.

Someone points out the small African violet sent by the schoolteacher's school. "Labor of love," I hear someone whisper to another.

Our grandmother had four children: a son who died in World War II; a daughter, who moved off the farm the first chance she got; and two sons, who never lived farther than an acre from the house they were born in. We are the descendants of the three surviving siblings.

Let me tell you about Grandmother's two sons, Ray (my father) and Ervin (my uncle). Someone in town once described the two brothers this way: If you drive your car into the ditch and call Ray to pull you out, he'd curse and holler at

4

you and he'd never let you forget it. "Oh, for Christ's sake, ain't you smart enough to look where you're going?" he'd say when you called him. And for the rest of your life he'd talk in your presence about the idiot (you) who went into the ditch in front of Eureka Bridge in broad daylight when the road wasn't even wet.

Still, he'd get there three minutes after you called him; he'd pull you out (cursing incessantly), but he'd do it quickly and you'd both be on your way.

Now Ervin was another matter. Call him to pull you out of a ditch and he'd say, "You bet. You just wait right there and I'll be along."

Meanwhile, he'd finish his coffee. He'd stop on the way to chat with a neighbor, and when he'd get there he might have forgotten a chain or something. "I'll be right back," he'd say, and you'd know you were in for another hour of sitting in the hot sun. It might take him a while to get you out, but he'd never mention it again.

A schoolteacher once said this about Ervin: "If you told him to do the fifty-yard dash, and gave him an afternoon to do it, he just *might* get it done."

Which is not to say that Ervin was lazy. He would get you out of the ditch, just as he'd plow and plant and spray and harvest. But things just took Ervin a little longer, like an old dog that circles around and around his spot before he finally lies down for a nap. Ervin got things done, but on Ervin's time.

Ervin and his wife had six children; he loved a house full of kids, they say. My mom and dad, more frugally, had just three.

Easter Sundays would see every one of Ervin's children in brand-new dresses and suits and squeaky new shoes, while our family wore hand-me-downs. "It's like Ervin must've been sleeping during the depression," my father once said. "The man doesn't know what it means to save a buck."

Ervin and Dad were a farming partnership almost all their

lives; Dad was the businessman, keeping the accounts, knowing when to sell, when to borrow, when to pay back, and when to set crops aside for a season. Ervin was the one who stayed up with the sows giving birth, making sure they didn't smother their offspring, making sure the runts got a chance. They say no one took better care of his animals than Ervin.

Dad could lie on the screen porch for about five minutes before he'd think of the next thing to do, before he might look up at the shiny coat of steel-gray paint on the ceiling and notice a chip, get out a ladder, scrape it smooth, and paint it over that same afternoon.

Ervin. Well, Ervin could lie on the screen porch in the gentle June breeze, look up toward the ceiling, and never even see it.

When our grandfather died in the 1970s, Dad and Ervin decided to split up their farming partnership. I suppose I don't have to tell you which brother lost his farm during the farm crisis of the 1980s.

As for Dad, this is his last year in farming; he's putting in his final harvest this season. He's quitting while he's ahead, retiring, you might say.

Of the eleven cousins, only one of us—one of Ervin's sons—went into farming. The rest of us are all of varying minds about our nostalgia for the farm. When we begin to be saddened by its empty buildings, the lack of bustle, we must always remind ourselves that even when this life could have been a choice, it was not a choice we made. As for Mitch, the cousin who went into farming, he's barely making it, losing his land little by little and working at a farm machinery factory in winters just to get by. We all know we were fiscally lucky to get out when we did.

The question has come up about what to do with Grandmother's house. No one has lived in it for almost two years, since at the age of ninety-nine she was finally put into a nursing home. Over phone wires from around the country, we discussed it dreamily; once there were half a dozen of us on one conference call, talking of how we could all chip in and fix it up, then take turns using it as our country retreat. We imagined sitting on the screen porch where so many of us have sat, pitting cherries, husking corn, or looking up at the ceiling and never seeing it.

But after we got off the phone, our exuberance waned. We admitted later that our fantasy of the country retreat faded into what it would really be like. You see, it would be all too quiet now; we'd look outside at the land cultivated by people we did not know and surely we would be thinking of those other days, back when the farm was alive with livestock and abuzz with machinery and the din of three families working; back when you'd hear the clanging of the feed traps on the feed bins, the hum of the water pump in the middle of the night.

Knock down the defunct buildings, renovate the old house, and you'd have a nice quiet country hamlet for some-one in the city. But not for any of us.

The rooms of Ervin's and my father's houses are filled with all of the cousins and our offspring; even Grandmother's sagging little home is full. I managed to light Grandmother's old gas stove; my cousin Susan fries up some eggs for break-fast and feeds all who drop by. We talk of the revolving door that was Grandmother's kitchen in the summer mornings; you never knew who would show up for breakfast or a cup of coffee before heading out to the fields. We remember how she used to fry dozens of eggs, not even trying to guess how many would come; any leftovers went to the cats in the barn.

Susan sets the table with dishes that have been faded and cracked through the ages, dull flatware, and chipped glasses. We grew up with this set of tableware, witnessed its demise, and it never occurred to us that Grandmother should replace it as it aged—just as today it would never occur to us to keep

7

faded and cracked dishes in our bright and gleaming new homes.

As we hold our mismatched china cups and saucers and talk, we hear, too, the creaks and the groans of the old house coming alive with a little attention, warming and softening to its first overnight guests in two years.

I must tell you, too, of my aunt Sally, the daughter of my grandmother. Sally, like most of us in the generation after her, left the farm when she was seventeen, just out of high school. She's lived in Fort Dodge, Minneapolis, Cedar Falls, Des Moines, and has been through a series of sales clerk and secretarial jobs, motherhood, and widowhood.

Still, she was never far from the rest of the family, never spent more than two weeks without a visit. She took her two daughters, Susan and Lynn, for entire summer months to live with the rest of us on the farm.

It was Sally who took care of our grandmother during the last years, Sally who moved into the old house to live with her mother. It was Sally who had refused everyone's advice to put Grandmother in the home until finally a day came when she fell and Sally could not lift her up and had to sit with her on the floor until help arrived.

And then it was Sally who drove from Fort Dodge at least twice a week to visit Grandmother, spending long hours in her stale-smelling room, trying to make conversation, reading to her, wheeling her outside for the warmth of the last few rays of summer sun. It was Sally who continued to come even after Grandmother became, at the age of a hundred and one, incontinent, belligerent, and sick of everything and everyone, including Sally.

Two days ago Susan flew to Des Moines from Denver. She tells of Sally picking her up at the airport, how her mother couldn't stop crying on the way from Des Moines to the farm. "Today is the first day in my life without her," Sally had said to Susan.

"I thought Mom would have been somewhat relieved," Susan tells me. "After all these years caretaking and watching the old woman's decline, she should be glad it's over. But the whole way here, she just kept crying and crying. I said to Mom, 'You should have no regrets. You took such good care of her all her life.'"

Susan sits in the kitchen chair that Grandmother used to call her "lookout chair," where she used to watch the comings and goings of the men and the hired hands while shelling peas or embroidering tea towels. Now Susan sits, looking outside at the empty barn with its broken windows. "I wanted to say to my mother, there and then, that I promise to take such good care of her."

"You will, when she needs it," I say.

"But I didn't say it. I couldn't. Because I know that tomorrow I'm getting back on a plane and heading to a town where Mom knows no one, that Mom would never move there and I would never move back here, so how could I make such a promise?"

Susan's sister, Lynn, comes down from where she's been sleeping upstairs; she's dressed in a bathrobe, eyes puffy and red; her nose swollen from a fever and flu that are now bronchitis. She tells of how last night her mother, always the caretaker, ran a hot bath in Grandmother's rusty bathtub to ease the chills; how she found some salts to soften the hard well water.

"In the middle of the night I had a fit of coughing," Lynn says, "and Mom came in with a hot drink and a vaporizer and made me breathe the steam. She took my temperature with her cool hand on my forehead, like she used to. I can't remember the last time someone's done that."

The next day: a swarm of relatives, friends. A reunion of sorts. An elderly cousin of our grandmother's who lives just the other side of town comes over with a large crock of beef and noodles for our lunch. She tells us, "I brought them here twenty years ago for your grandpa's funeral. Your grandmother liked them so much she asked me to bring them over when she died. So here they are."

I take a walk around the farm with my cousin Margaret, the schoolteacher. We come upon the corncrib, recalling that the structure had been finished the very day Ervin, her father, was born. She traces her finger along the date, which our grandfather had written into the cement that spring day of 1931. We sit and listen to the wind race through the beaten-up building. We can hardly picture it bulging with corn; we hardly remember that it was once our glorious spaceship taking us to another planet.

Later, across the field I sit in the kitchen with Ervin's wife, June, and their son Ben. Ben and I are the same age; we grew up like brothers until we both moved away after high school.

Things are not going so well for Ben these days. His second marriage is failing, and his kids are in more than the usual teenage trouble. He hates his job in Dallas.

And though he has told me these things and more, he has not mentioned them to his mother, for he knows that June has troubles of her own.

Ben, like most of us, never wanted to stay in this little town. But he does not enjoy coming home to witness its defeat. He does not like seeing his brother Mitch losing everything and working winters at a factory. He does not like to see his father, now in his sixties, embarking on a new career of driving trucks across the country. He does not like to see his mother slinging hamburgers at a local chain-operated truck stop. Part of him wonders if there was anything in his life he could have done to make it all turn out differently—a wonder we have all had from time to time.

Although he is not complaining to his mother about his own life, he is saying that it is shit, her having to wait tables in her sixties when she should be tending a garden and doing what she loves, taking her husband their lunches in the fields, canning, sewing, fixing, making stupid dolls we all made fun of as kids but that won all sorts of silly ribbons at county fairs.

"It wasn't easy work, what you did," Ben is saying, "but whatever you did it was yours, and it just has to beat serving mass-produced food to strangers on the highway."

He goes on and he asks her: What's it like, waking up to an empty house? Do you hear the echoes of your six children, screaming and laughing and fighting as we got ready for the school bus? And when you brought each of us into the world, did you ever imagine that you'd only see us once or twice a year? Yes, it was more at first when we moved just to Waterloo, Fort Dodge, Cedar Rapids, but it's less often now that we've moved on elsewhere.

"Something's lost," Ben continues, "and I'm not sure whose fault it is. Maybe it's ours for leaving in the first place, but aren't you tired of waking up alone, making your toast and coffee (remember the big breakfasts we'd all have?), and driving your car into town by yourself (remember when going to town was a big deal?)? But you don't stop at the boarded-up stores in the square. You drive out to a shiny new truck stop on the highway, across from the Wal-Mart, and you serve food to strangers who are in a hurry to speed elsewhere because if they don't get to wherever they're going first, someone else will—"

"Enough," his mother says, putting her coffee mug down. "I see it a little differently, I suppose. Because you know what I do every morning before I go wait tables? I get ready and I put on my uniform and I have a cup of coffee and then I give myself fifteen minutes just to relax and look out the window. I still love the view out there, even if the land isn't ours any-more. I say a tiny prayer thanking God for my legs and my arms and my eyes and I pray for him to help Ervin come home safe and for him to help me do a good job at work that day. I pray that I won't screw up the orders, that I won't drop a tray full of dishes, that I won't yell at the cook and he won't yell at me. And at the end of the day if all's gone well, I say thank you very much, my cup runneth over. And if it does not go well, I pray that he will help me do better tomorrow. Now that I've listened to your little rant and rave, Ben, I shall say another prayer. I will pray that you will find such peace in your life."

Ben looks down at his fingernails and begins picking at them, though there's nothing to clean. He looks at me, shrugs, and says, "Well, cousin, what can we say to that?"

The funeral. A windy bright day—Indian summer.

As we file past the open casket Margaret says, "One hundred and one years. It should seem like a long time, but somehow I thought she'd live forever."

At the cemetery the sun is so bright you have to squint to see. More than one of us has to tell our children not to put on sunglasses. The wind is so strong that the minister's voice can scarcely be heard above the flapping of the canopy over the grave.

The wind is so strong. Strong enough to carry an old soul home.

After the funeral, Grandmother's house is full. The front yard becomes a parking lot; inside and on the porch, women serve coffee and cake on Grandmother's old best blue dishes while men stand outside in their suits, smoking cigarettes and talking of very old times.

I sit with an elderly man. He's nearly deaf; he walks with a cane—barely. He's one of those people I'd see in town many times when I was a child, but I can't quite remember who he is, so I ask.

"I'm Melvin Hyde," he says. He knows who I am. "Your grandmother saw me come into this world eighty-two years ago when she was the hired girl at my folks' house."

As it turns out, in two weeks, this man, too, is dead.

That night, all the visitors gone, Aunt Sally's family and ours sit around Grandmother's old oak table and eat a supper of casseroles that friends and neighbors have brought by. It is my cousin Susan's husband who looks up and sees them, a few sheep grazing in the front yard.

"Do people always let sheep wander around in their yards like that?" he asks. He, of course, wouldn't know, this being his first time on the farm.

We go to the window and we see about two dozen sheep peacefully munching on the grass and on what's left of Grandmother's old flower garden. The flock belongs to a neighboring farmer; they've gotten out, somehow, from the pasture that my father had rented to the neighbor.

Soon, we're all outside, planning a strategy. "Okay, you go on that side. We'll stay here . . ." But as we try to encircle the sheep, the animals move out through the gap.

Across the field, from Ervin's nearby house, Ervin's kids come running, laughing, and soon they too attempt to encircle the sheep. It isn't long until there are more cousins and our children than there are sheep. But like horses that can sense fear, the sheep sense our incompetence; they know a real shepherd when they see one and we aren't it. Instead of running as a herd, they scatter—some onto the road, others on up the path to Ervin's yard.

Now, with twice as many people as sheep, we form a line behind them, our hands linked like we're playing the children's game Red Rover. Slowly, finally, we form a half circle around the sheep; we ease them back in through the gate that someone holds open.

Sweating, laughing, we stand talking for a while, our hearts beating from the chase. We agree not to tell my father about our adventure. "Ray would never let us forget how the sheep almost outsmarted us," we say.

That night, even the World Series, playing on television in its last game, can't hold us.

Outside, the moon is full, a harvest moon, so bright and clear that we can see our shadows.

Our youngest cousin—the baby of the family—stops in front of the old barn where the slant of the moon casts her eerie shadow. She does a gentle arabesque in the moonlight, and the shadow of the tip of her finger stretches to the empty hayloft. Soon, she and her older sisters and my sisters and all the women are dancing, their graceful figures making odd, angular, and almost frightfully tall stick figures against the dark wall of the barn.

Across the dark night we see the headlamps of my father's combine as he drives through the field in a hurry to get in his last harvest before tomorrow's rains. We hear the distant hum.

The next day is all drizzle and cold; gone is the glaring Indian summer. It is the true beginning of winter.

One by one, cars pull out of the muddy driveway as we wave our good-byes to each other through the rain. Most of us are heading to Des Moines or Minneapolis to take jets in different directions: Denver, Dallas, New York, Atlanta, and elsewhere.

As I ascend into the sky, before I'm above the clouds I look down the miles of dark fields below with their tiny specks of worn-out buildings. I think of Aunt Sally, with no one to take care of, and I think of Uncle Ervin, tomorrow driving his truck who knows where, and I think of my father driving his final truckload to the co-op.

And I think, too, of the next generation, my cousins and myself—we who can hardly miss what we're leaving because it's not really there anymore. We have convinced ourselves

14

that change is a part of every generation, every life; we understand where we fall in this inevitability. We know full well that the future belongs to those who refuse to sit still for five minutes, so off we go. But as we rush back to our lives in the cities, each of us must wonder, in our own ways, how much longer someone will remember to bring beef and noodles to the next family funeral. Or how long it will be before someone will touch our feverish foreheads with a cool hand. Or if we'll ever again see our sisters dance together by the light of the harvest moon.

THE HEALTH FOOD JUNKIE JUICE AND SANDWICH BAR

A week after I graduated from high school, I started looking for a summer job. "Arnie Rosen'll hire you," my father told me. But I was looking for something new in the world, and not much interested in Rosen's Ladies' Apparel, that downtown dinosaur across from my dad's coffee shop, with its eight floors devoted to yesterday's woman: jewelry and cosmetics on one, then shoes, millenary, cruise wear, lingerie, evening gowns, furs, and a tearoom on top. I just couldn't see myself as a colleague to white-gloved elevator operators and beaky salesladies, doused in Shalimar and dressed in Leslie Fay.

"Maybe next summer," I told my dad, and I headed to the other side of town for an interview at the Health Food Junkie Juice and Sandwich Bar. I waited for my interview with about a dozen other applicants—thin, earthy girls with butt-length hair, all dressed in patched blue jeans and thongs, all smoking cigarettes and reading newspapers I'd never heard of. Sitting there in my half-serious, working-girl A-line skirt, stockings, and sensible shoes, I thought that maybe I didn't fit in so well there, either.

When I told my father I got the job, he was not impressed. "Marci," he said, "if all you're going to do is sling hash, you might as well come work for me." Until that moment I hadn't really thought of the Health Food Junkie Juice and Sandwich Bar as a mere hash house, not along the lines of my dad's coffee shop, anyway. Though I wasn't sure what the Health Food Junkie Juice and Sandwich Bar was, if not a restaurant, I knew that doing dishes there would have little in common with serving hamburgers to businessmen downtown.

On my first night of work, Greg, the co-owner, showed me around his little two-room restaurant, which he had converted from a former neighborhood hardware store. It still had the old wooden floors and vaulted ceilings; Greg had hung leafy plants in the storefront windows. The front room was a dining room, with mismatched wooden chairs and tables, an orange piano, and a jungle mural on the wall. The kitchen area, where Greg worked, was behind a counter where he took the orders. My station was in the back room, with its dishwasher, ovens, sinks, and the walk-in refrigerator.

The little round metal dishwasher seemed tiny next to the precariously stacked dish racks full of dirty dishes towering over it. "I'm a little behind," he said, motioning around him. Every available space was overtaken with full dish tubs. My dad, a former cook in the navy, would've had a stroke. He never ever wanted more than two racks of dishes piled up at a time. "More than two stacks, and you're in the weeds," Dad would say. "In the weeds" was what the waitresses and cooks and dishwashers called it when they got swamped during the rush, when the orders would get backed up and you'd run out of clean silverware, out of the special, and you'd bring the orders to the wrong table and a few customers would keep asking "How much longer?" while some old lady would say her hamburger wasn't done enough.

Now it looked to me like Greg was already swamped, and the evening rush hadn't even begun. "Let me get started," I offered, wondering where to begin. There were dish tubs on the floor under the pizza ovens, on top of the refrigerator. "What do you need most?" I asked, trying to be systematic about it.

"Let's have a little welcome beverage first, Marci," Greg said. He opened the door of the walk-in cooler, where there were more dirty dishes on the floor. "How 'bout a malted yeast?" he called from inside.

"Sure," I said. He was, after all, my boss.

He walked out of the cooler and handed me a beer. "Cheers," he said, but then the string of brass bells on the front door jingled, and a group of customers came in. "Make yourself at home," he said as he walked out front.

I thought he was making fun of me. I stood there among all those dishes in that filthy room, and suddenly Rosen's Ladies' Apparel sounded pretty good to me. I wondered if it was too late to have Dad talk to Arnie Rosen.

As it turned out, Greg's dishwasher wasn't too hard to figure out; it was a one-person, three-rack operation, wedged between the ovens and the walk-in. The wash cycle took four minutes, about the time it took to rinse and load the oncoming rack, then unload the rack of drying dishes. I managed to get caught up. I had, after all, filled in now and then at my dad's coffee shop when a dishwasher was sent home, drunk.

I think it was busier that night than even Greg had anticipated; people sat on the window ledges, reading newspapers and waiting for tables while Greg took orders, prepared them, and served them to the customers.

"Is there something else I can do, Greg?" I asked. "Are you in the weeds?"

Thinking I must have said something like, "Are you into weed," he looked at me through his rimless glasses, confused. "No," he said. "No, but feel free, Marci. In the back room, if you want."

I didn't get the chance to explain what I meant until later.

He didn't say much to me during the two-hour rush except, "You catch on quick" and "You do good work." I wasn't impressed. I knew how restaurant management says those things to keep the help moving right along. I vowed to finish my shift that night and never come back to the Health Food Junkie Juice and Sandwich Bar, with its flies buzzing around and piles of dishes, with its owner who didn't even know how to speak the language of restaurants, let alone run one.

But later, after the customers had all gone home and we had cleaned up for the night, Greg and I sat in the dining room, drinking a beer. I was going to tell him then that this just wasn't for me, but he said, as he wiped off his glasses and looked at me with fuzzy hazel eyes, "You know why I hired you, Marci?"

"Why?" I truly had no idea. Maybe those other girls with butt-length hair had criminal records, but I didn't think that would bother Greg so much.

"Because when I saw you sitting there next to all those other women, you seemed so *yourself*. Those others, I knew that they would think it would be so very cool to work here, but in about a week they'd be too cool to do dishes. No one likes to do dishes, Marci, but you don't take it personally, I can tell. You know who you are and you know what matters."

On the way home I had to laugh. Since when did I know what mattered? Back then, nothing held me. By my senior year, I had already taken up and dropped the violin, the clarinet, the piano, and a couple of boyfriends. I had joined and quit the debate and swim teams and the marching band. I had worked at my dad's coffee shop now and then, and of course I hated that. I still wasn't sure which college I was going to that fall; I had my money down on two.

My mother was always telling me that I was flopping around like a fish out of water, but then here was Greg telling me that I knew who I was and what mattered. So of course I went back to his restaurant the next night, just to see what this was all about.

I imagined that Greg had blown into Des Moines from some wonderful elsewhere, a coast or somewhere like Duluth or Canada. But a few nights later over our nightly beer in the dark, candlelit dining room at the end of our shift, I learned that Greg was just a small-town boy from southern Iowa, where his dad operated a grain elevator. He got the idea for the restaurant when he was stationed in California during the service.

"The service?" I had asked. It hadn't occurred to me that Greg could have been in the military.

"I was only in it for a few months," Greg said. "I got discharged early."

I was too polite to ask what for, but he knew I wanted to know.

"A stupid accident, Marci," he said. "I burned half my face off."

I tried to look at him closer, but I couldn't see it.

"It's behind the beard, Marci," he said, blushing, self-consciously covering his neck and chin with both his hands. "It's not as bad as it was." I could see it now, some shiny pink skin near his ears and below his hairline.

"At least it kept you out of Vietnam," I said. He didn't answer.

"I mean, that's something," I said.

"I suppose," he answered, still rubbing his hands through his long, full, golden-brown beard.

Though I didn't think about it that summer, I've often wondered since how old Greg was then; when you're seventeen, anyone over twenty-five is about the same age. He seemed around thirty, but then, a full beard can make a young man look so much older. He was, I guess, somewhere in that nowhere land between my own flop-around youth and my parents' settled middle age.

I often wonder, too, if wherever he is he still wears a full beard to hide that patch of pink scarred flesh.

It wasn't long before I got Greg to let me work the counter. Why should I stand there, caught up and reading alternative newspapers while he was in the weeds? I learned how to run the veggies through the Champion juicer, how to make apple butter and bean spread, and sautéed vegetable sandwiches.

The Health Food Junkie Juice and Sandwich Bar was a world away from my dad's coffee shop. Dad's coffee shop was known for its good, homey, made-from-scratch food served with almost fast-food efficiency. At Greg's place, everything was made from scratch, too, but no one was in any hurry. The customers would linger for hours, improvising on the piano or reading three-week-old copies of the *Village Voice,* sipping grassy tea. I liked the way when it got slow Greg and I would just sit around and shoot the breeze, thinking up new dishes to make, compiling new tapes of music to play.

My dad—and every other restaurant manager in the world besides Greg—would always say, "Got time to lean, got time to clean." And though Greg's back room could have used a few more frequent scrub downs, when I'd offer, he'd say he'd do it tomorrow, in the midafternoon when I wasn't around. Of course, it rarely got done. Instead, Greg would get caught up in a conversation with a customer, or negotiate with an artist who wanted to hang her pictures on our walls or an old musical-instruments maker who wanted to display his wooden flutes in our window.

During the months I worked at the Health Food Junkie Juice and Sandwich Bar, my father would often shake his head and warn me: "Once a hash slinger, always a hash slinger." My mother, who was his noontime cashier, would say, "Marci, it's no business to be in."

"It's not regular hash slinging, Dad."

"You feed people, they pay you," he said. "You've got dishwashers and busboys and waitresses and bosses and customers you gotta please. It's a restaurant."

I'd try to explain how it was different. I told him how there weren't really any waitresses. Greg took the orders, then he and I would cook them up and serve them. When I was both dishwasher and busgirl, sometimes the customers would bring the dishes back themselves to the dish room, just to say hi to me.

"The clientele's different, Dad," I said. "And at least I don't have to deal with the old biddies you deal with."

"Those old biddies paid for the braces on your teeth."

But Dad knew how I felt about his customers, that I never could seem to care whether someone was in a hurry or if I'd given them a short soupspoon instead of a long-handled ice cream spoon for their malt or even if their hamburger was too rare. I could wash dishes, I could help out in the kitchen, but what I could not do was to believe, like my father did, that the customer was always right. It was not only untrue, it was annoying.

I switched tactics. I tried to explain to my father how Greg would say, "If you see anyone try to walk out without paying, let them go. They need the food more than I need the money."

"You can't feed all the bums in the world, Marci," Dad said.

"That's not the way Greg sees it," I told him. "Because all the bums in the world don't come to your door."

Dad put down his newspaper and rolled his eyes. "You'll never get anywhere hash slinging for those beatniks," he said.

And though I knew that all the bums in Des Moines knew they could get a free lunch now and then at my father's coffee shop, that my dad was really a soft touch too, I didn't press the point. Why call attention to the Health Food Junkie Juice and Sandwich Bar? Why go on and on about how the clientele was much more interesting, the decorations livelier, how if I had time to lean, I could just lean? Why tell him that I was falling a little in love with the joint, with the dusty flutes in the window that no one bought, the mismatched wooden chairs, this pocket of ease that defied the workaday wisdom of my father.

The last thing I wanted was for Mom and Dad to drop by for a cup of coffee to see this wonderful place for themselves. There'd be piles of dirty dishes all over the counters, a guy playing not-so-melodic music on the orange piano. There'd be dusty, wilting plants in the window, and we didn't serve anything that had caffeine.

Besides, I liked to think of my dad's coffee shop and the Health Food Junkie Juice and Sandwich Bar as two parallel universes, two separate, never-intersecting worlds. It was fine if some people wanted to live in the world where businessmen grabbed toast and coffee in the morning and shop clerks took breaks for pie and tea, but I preferred that other world, where there was no time clock and plenty of time, where Greg would say to me every two weeks, "How much do you think I owe you?" I was young. I could imagine that one place had nothing to do with another and that there was plenty of room in our world for both.

The day my little worlds met up was a day like any other. Greg had just stepped out to run an errand, and the rush began before he got back. There I was, taking orders, trying to cook and serve them as more and more people kept coming in. As usual, no one seemed to be in a great big hurry, but still I was confused—in the weeds—trying to sauté vegetables, make fresh juices, and throw together salads, stay on track while more people came up to the counter and the phone rang and rang.

I was running some carrots through the juicer when I saw her come in—one of those dime-tipping, finger-snapping, eggs-over-medium-but-not-too-hard-bacon-crisp, Miss-this-coffee's-cold kind of ladies. I saw her walk in and look around reluctantly—sniffing, I swear, at the clientele, at the dust

24

visible in the setting sun's light through the front windows. She was looking around like she had expected the tearoom on the top floor of Rosen's Ladies' Apparel.

I continued to prepare the orders while she looked at the menu on the chalkboard.

Finally she said, "Miss, I'm a little in a hurry. Would you mind taking my order?"

I had not been called "Miss" since my ill-fated waitressing attempts at Dad's place. "Miss" was usually what they called you when you'd walk by with a tray full of food and they'd decide that that was the moment to ask for more coffee, rather than when you'd walked by—a minute earlier—with the pot.

"Have you decided on something?" I asked.

Our menu could seem a little foreign to the uninitiated, with items like tofu and bulgur and sesame. Even the more normal dishes had strange names, like "Bob's Big Bash," described only in small print as a grilled cheese sandwich on homemade whole-grain bread. I knew this lady was probably wondering why she had stopped here in the first place. Probably some bridge partner of hers, one of the younger ones who macraméed, decoupaged, cooked Indian, and was into any other streamlined, watered-down hippie fad, had told this lady about this hip new vegetarian restaurant, and now this lady, in her close-fitting hound's-tooth check suit, was standing there, wondering what was so great about this place.

She took her time asking questions about the menu. She wanted to know what the difference was between bean sprouts and alfalfa sprouts, and exactly what spices we put in our avocado-spread sandwich. She kept asking me these questions, as if the dining room weren't full of people, as if I didn't have ten orders tacked on the order board right in front of her face.

"I suppose I could have a tuna-fish sandwich," she said,

"on white toast, well done, white toast. How long do you think that will be?"

I put down a bean-spread sandwich I had ready to take out and I looked right at her. "We do not serve tuna fish," I said. "We are a vegetarian restaurant."

"I am well aware of that," she said. "But I know vegetarians who eat fish."

"Not here they don't," I said. I took the sandwich out to the customer. When I got back, she asked, "Well, then. What would you suggest?"

Here's what my father would have done: He'd have said, "Tell me what you like and I'll make it for you."

Here's what I did: I suggested a raw tofu sandwich and a glass of cabbage-yeast juice.

"What, exactly, is tofu?" she asked.

I opened the cooler, brought out a big carton of the white stuff, fished a slab out with a fork and displayed it in front of her. "This is tofu, ma'am."

"Oh," she said, wrinkling up her nose. "I wouldn't feed that to my dog." She straightened her short-waisted jacket, turned, and walked away like she couldn't get out that door fast enough.

It was only then that I saw that Greg had come in through the back room. "What was that all about?" he asked.

"Guess she doesn't like tofu," I answered. "Did you hear?"

"Yes, I heard that, Marci. But we have other things. Why didn't you suggest the sautéed vegetables, or the grilled cheese sandwich? And everyone likes pineapple-coconut juice."

"Yeah, but she wanted—tuna fish!" I said, hoping this might soften his glare.

Greg looked around at the half-cooked orders and the

tickets all lined up. He lowered his voice. "And what did you tell her?" he asked.

"I should have told her I'm just sure we serve tuna fish."

"But what *did* you tell her?"

"Look, she was in the wrong place," I said. "What did you want me to do?"

He put down his sack of groceries, looked straight ahead of me, trembling as he leaned on his hands. "Walk across the street and buy her a steak if she wanted one," he answered.

I thought of my dad and how if something was sent back to the kitchen he'd make it again and again if it wasn't quite right. He didn't like doing it; he'd mutter words under his breath. He'd bring the dish out, place it in front of a woman who would look at it like it was something dirty. Still, he'd say, "You let me know, now, if that's the way you like it, ma'am. I got all day to get it right." I hated the way he acted so dumb.

A few people in the dining room were glancing at us; a man with long white hair came up and asked if his green bean pizza would be coming up soon. I started to take a tub of dishes to the next room, but Greg stopped me. "Why don't you take tonight off," he said.

"You mean I'm fired?"

"No, but it might be best if you weren't here right now."

I walked slowly back to the dish room and got my purse, taking my time, hoping he'd come back and tell me he'd changed his mind. He didn't.

I drove around that evening, just wanting to get lost for a while. I thought of heading west, straight through the suburbs and out of town, but when I got to a main street, I turned east, winding through some old neighborhoods with curvy roads. Again and again I tried to convince myself that she was just some old biddy, but Greg's anger kept coming back to me.

I found myself downtown, where the streets were dark

and quiet. It was that time in the city's history when the downtown was a ghost town at night; right after all the theaters and the cocktail lounges with flashing neon martini glasses had closed for good, a few years before the warehouse district was renovated with its bright Mexican restaurants and trendy spaghetti joints.

I drove slowly by the dark windows of Dad's coffee shop, with its neon aqua nightlights burning softly behind the counter. The place hadn't been changed since he bought it a few years before I was born. I stopped the car and I went up to the windows and looked inside at the smooth, clean countertops and the shiny chrome tables. If it were still there today, people now would think it was chic in a 1950s retro way, but that night it just looked old. Still, I remember thinking then that he had done a good job with it, and for the first of many times in my life, I wondered why hash slinging had been such a defeat for him. I knew that if I ever did get out of hash slinging, it wouldn't be because I was so very clever, but mostly because I wasn't that good at it.

As I got back into my car I looked across the street at Rosen's Ladies' Apparel. In the window were dozens of colorful wide-brimmed hats (Arnie always thought hats would make a comeback). On an easel in the center of the cheerful display, a large, block-lettered sign said, "Hat Sale." The sign had been there all summer.

I had to talk to Greg. When I got on the freeway, I looked back toward old downtown, where a few lights glimmered dully. Up ahead of me, the western suburbs cast a domed glow like a new planet.

The old neighborhood was quiet; the lights were off at the Health Food Junkie Juice and Sandwich Bar. I drove over to Greg's house, a few blocks away. His car was in the gravel driveway, a faint light shone from an upstairs window. I tapped lightly on the door, not really loud enough for anyone to hear, and it eased open. I let myself in.

His was a funny old house—it reminded me of some aging aunt's place, with heavy curtains and valences and thick braided rugs, figurines and books on the window ledges and mantle. I thought, for a moment, of that woman I had been so rude to, but already that seemed ages ago. I sat in a dusty overstuffed chair, looking out the window at the dark, starless night and wondering what would happen next.

I got up and walked as quietly as I could up the stairs. I had only been to Greg's house once, to a bon voyage party for his silent partner, who was taking off for Europe that summer. I walked on the creaky floors covered with thin woven rugs toward the room with the faint light.

There was a soft breeze coming through the open window, lifting the sheer curtains above his mattress on the floor. He was lying there, with a book open facedown on his chest, his head turned to the wall. I leaned on the door frame with my arms crossed and looked on.

He began to slowly turn and stretch, but then paused and opened his eyes. Lifting up his head, he took in a sharp, scared breath, but then he lay back down and muttered, "Marci." He exhaled slowly and swallowed, then bent his elbow over his eyes and turned his head to the wall.

I stood there for a few minutes longer; then I lay down with him, pulled an old quilt over us, and slept with him until morning, happy, for once, to be right where I was.

One late afternoon the spring I was ten years old, my mother was driving me through town on the way home from one of my music lessons. I don't recall if it was the violin or the clarinet or the piano I was studying at this time, but I remember we were late coming home; she had something in the oven on a timer. So when the signals at the railroad intersection started flashing and the gate came down before we could cross the tracks, Mother said, "Damn."

As she sat back and watched the train go by, she realized something. "What do you know," she said. "That's it, Marci. That's the five-oh-five, and the last time a passenger train will come through Des Moines. I read about it in this morning's paper." She got out, stood between the car seat and the doors, and waved at the four or five passengers in each car, who for a moment looked strangely back at her through the green-tinted windows, then, understanding, waved back.

I suppose that's how I felt those last few weeks in the summer of 1977 working at the Health Food Junkie Juice and Sandwich Bar. I knew its time was up even before a guy with spiky purple hair came in one night and banged on the piano with beheaded Barbie dolls, even before a clean-cut bill collector—who looked about my age—came by, rolled his eyes at us, and told Greg to get a job. Its time was up, you could feel it in the air. Still, I felt like those passengers on that last 5:05 bound for Omaha must have felt, knowing that it was the last train, but happy just to be on it.

Three weeks before I was to go off to college, my father honked his horn at me as I was pulling out of the driveway on my way to work. He was just getting home.

He rolled down his window. "Marci," he said, "the word is that those beatniks you work for haven't been paying their taxes. They'll be shut down any day."

I didn't ask him how he knew; I didn't tell him that I knew, too, what he and Greg and everyone else knew: that the Health Food Junkie Juice and Sandwich Bar's time was just about up.

"Why don't you talk to Arnie Rosen?" Dad said. "He told me he'd hire you for August inventory."

"'Maybe next summer, Dad," I said, backing up, screeching out the driveway and through town to the Health Food Junkie Juice and Sandwich Bar, where the air-conditioning was broken, where Greg and I sat in the walk-in cooler and drank sweet, cold pineapple-coconut juice.

I never did get to work for Arnie Rosen. That year while I was at college, Rosen's Ladies' Apparel went bankrupt. While other downtown retailers had cut their losses and moved out a few years before, Arnie's store had become an obsession for him. Dad says he ordered inventory and kept his sales staff like it was still 1966, confident that he could, like his father and uncles before him, ride out any adverse trend. He lost everything, for when the banks refused him more credit, he cashed in his own stocks, went into his own savings to keep paying his bills.

Dad's street-level coffee shop wasn't doing so great, as the skywalks were being built, rerouting the lunchtime crowds. But Dad lucked out. A developer offered to buy his lease. The summer after my first year of school, Dad closed up, cashed in, and retired just in time. Greg's restaurant, too, was closed. Greg and his partner were traveling (or, my dad claimed, running from the IRS). At school that year I had gotten occasional postcards, first from the Southwest, then Mexico and Venezuela.

Once again, I needed a summer job. A swanky private dining club was hiring, and though I still wasn't fully enamored with waiting tables, by now I knew it was only temporary, a path to something else. When I told my dad I got the job at the club, I thought he'd be somewhat impressed. It was, after all, a nice place, where I learned French service, tableside cooking, and got paid three times as much as he or Greg could ever pay. But Dad just shrugged his shoulders and said, "The king's dog is the king of dogs."

As I was getting ready to go to work one hot August day, Greg called from a place called Porlamar. "I've got a minute's worth of bolivars to tell you how much you'd love it here," he said, going on to describe this landscape of a desert by the ocean, the orange-and-blue fishing boats, and the ruins of the Spanish fortess. I wasn't sure whether his call was an invitation. I tried not to wonder how he was making his money these days. I wanted to ask him if he were really a fugitive, but the line cracked and he said a quick good-bye that lingered like an echo in a tunnel a few seconds after we were disconnected.

One late August night the last summer I lived in Des Moines, the summer before I graduated from college, moved elsewhere, and got out of hash slinging forever, I waited on Arnie Rosen and his wife. They had dropped their membership, but because they had belonged for forty-some-odd years, because they had, in better times, thrown a lobster luau each summer, they were offered honorary dining room privileges, though they didn't go out much.

He remembered that this would be my senior year in college; he asked me what I was studying. When I told him, he smiled and said, "I bet that makes your dad proud."

He asked me what the market price for lobster was that night. After I told him I watched him look over the menu through his thick glasses, adding up the prices, figuring in the drinks, the fifteen percent service charge all in his head, like only an old-school retailer can do.

His wife ordered the steak. "Medium—not too well, but pinkish. Baked potato, and please, Marci, have them take the foil off *before* they cut it open. I can't stand those little metal shavings in my potato."

Arnie ordered the chicken piccata, the cheapest thing on the menu.

I took his order into the kitchen, where the chef and sous-chef were arguing with the maître d', where we had run out of clean coffee cups and a captain was complaining that the romaine had freezer burn and a waitress was saying we didn't have the right kind of cherries for the cherries jubilee. But I wasn't paying much attention. I was thinking of Rosen's Ladies' Apparel, now converted into an office building, and I wondered what they did with the handcrafted latticework on the wrought iron front doors with its frilly "R." I wondered where those beaky Shalimar salesladies and white-gloved elevator operators were now. I hadn't seen them in the malls.

I handed Arnie's order to the chef, but then I snatched it back and said, "Wait, that's not right." I crossed out chicken piccata, and wrote in lobster Thermidor, which was stealing, I suppose, but I had to do something for Arnie Rosen, who had lost everything just trying to stand still while the rest of us moved unsteadily on.

GRANDFATHER'S LOAN, 1933

For this farmer, anyway, it's been a good year. Harvest over, Albert goes to town, taking with him all the money he owes the bank for his new barn—rebuilt after last year's fire—plus some extra for savings.

"Why don't you keep your money for now? Buy some hogs, Albert," the banker advises. "Couldn't you build another cistern? A new foundation for the hen house?"

Albert shakes his head, smiles at his old schoolmate the banker. "Cliff," he says, "I just don't like owing you money. And it's time I put something away."

"Not now, it isn't," the banker whispers, looking around, pushing the cash back toward him through the window. "You take this home. You think about it."

He takes the money home. He thinks about it. And with the immigrant's disdain for debt, he drives back to town with his money the next week.

But that day there's a crowd outside the bank, a sign he can't quite read in the window. He sees his brother Ott, who waves him over and says, "They've shut down, Albert. Hope you don't need any money."

MONSIEUR PHERLON

Monsieur Pherlon's love for Paris has never had anything to do with the literary. As he walks past the plaque on Gertrude Stein's former residence on the rue de Fleurus, he hardly gives her a thought. This is all he has to say about *that* generation: they knew a good thing when they saw one.

For the third morning of his trip, Monsieur sits in the little café in Montparnasse, writing postcards to former students back home.

"Chère Mademoiselle," he writes. "Me voilà à Paris . . ." Here I am in Paris. He wants to continue, telling her that he is just a few blocks from the Luxembourg Gardens, but he stops, knowing there is no perfect equivalent of *block,* no word to describe the errant curves of the streets, the nonangular intersections. Monsieur looks around. There are no sharp corners in this area of Montparnasse.

". . . à quelques pas des Jardins . . . ," he writes, a few steps from the gardens. Though it's not quite right either (he's about four blocks), it better describes the light-stepped, dreamlike way he stumbled here in the early, giddy stage of jet lag three days ago when he, by chance, came upon this most memorable little café.

What else is there to say? Monsieur wonders. He puts

down his pen and sips his green Vittel-menthe. The white-bloused, black-vested waiter places condiments on his table: salt, pepper, Dijon mustard, vinegar, and oil. The waiter has round glasses and thick wavy gray hair; in America he would be mistaken for an intellectual, Monsieur thinks. The waiter bustles about, fastidiously covering the tables with paper tablecloths and setting the glass containers on top, preventing the covers from flying off in the breeze. When he disappears, Monsieur imagines him inside, smoking Gitanes, drinking a *café exprès,* and arguing EEC politics with the barman.

It is only 10 A.M., two full hours until lunch. Monsieur has his morning all planned out: he'll finish his little green drink, have a beer, and write more postcards to former students back home. Then he'll spend at least an hour walking the streets, reading the menus of the day posted in the restaurant windows, choosing where to eat. He's planning on twenty-seven more mornings like this one, sitting in cafés, menu shopping, pondering the difference between things like *à quelques pas* and *a few blocks*. What a luxury!

This is the first summer in twenty years that Monsieur Pherlon has found himself in France, alone, with the time to think about how there is no common French equivalent for the word *block*. Usually during June, George Pherlon is a chaperon on the Woodrow Wilson High School French exchange trip. And because his method of chaperoning was rather laissez-faire, Monsieur often spent his trip keeping the fifteen students out of trouble, retrieving lost students from dubious areas of the city, persuading the police not to arrest some boys for jumping over the metro's turnstiles, apologizing to hotel concierges for wine bottles that were thrown out of third-story windows by students, some of whom are drunk for the first time ever.

"You must understand," Monsieur would explain to the would-be plaintiffs, "these youngsters are finding a joie de vivre for the first time in their lives. It can be a little overwhelming." Pherlon knows that the quickest way to a Frenchman's sensitive side is to tell him what he never grows tired of hearing: that only the French know how to live.

And so Monsieur sits, almost beside himself with anticipation. For this trip, he will not have to bail anyone out of trouble. He finally finishes his postcard to Sandra, a once-young ingenue he had years ago saved from a particularly groping, grasping, middle-aged Frenchman. "This year," he writes, "the only one I'll have to bail out of trouble is myself."

Monsieur Pherlon teaches high school French. He spends nine months a year teaching mostly from texts whose protagonists are named Robert and Marie-Ange, who find themselves in the same mundane situations as his students: in a school cafeteria, at a swimming pool, in a grocery store. As if the only difference between France and America were the language.

Inevitably, the students will get caught up with the words on the page.

"Monsieur Pherlon," the same type of towheaded debate team smart-aleck kid will ask every year, "how can a table be feminine? Huh? What's so feminine about a table?" The kid will think he's stumped the teacher; he'll think he's the only one in the history of the world who has ever pondered the purpose of gender in Romance languages. Monsieur's inability to answer the pupil's question doesn't bother him nearly as much as the fact that the young man wants French to be a direct translation of English.

Monsieur is less interested in teaching the students about the genders of nouns and the conjugations of verbs. No, as much as he can, without getting too far behind in the school district's curriculum, Monsieur will have them study the cultural aspects of France, a new topic every week: "The Grandes Dames de France"; "Those Kings Named Louis"; "Where Good Wine Comes From"; "The Great Cheeses of

France." Ten to fifteen minutes each day, Monsieur will describe details of the history and culture of France with rabid excitement, his round face and balding head flushing a bright pink as he gets in as much as he can before the bell rings.

"Monsieur," Monsieur calls to the waiter, for he knows it's gauche to call a waiter "*garçon.*"

"Oui, Monsieur," the waiter answers.

"Une bière s'il vous plaît." Pherlon is civil but not effusive with condescending politeness. He knows how to treat waiters.

"Being a waiter in France is a highly respected occupation," he always tells his students—a combination of rich, old-money kids from the area and the poorer kids bused in. Rich or poor, no one in any of his classes ever believes him. "And teaching," Pherlon will add, "teaching is very highly esteemed."

At this some of the richer kids will snicker. "Yeah, sure," he might hear a few say, for they know that Pherlon doesn't make enough on his teaching salary to afford his once-a-year trips to France. On the weekends he waits tables at a country club to which many of his students' parents belong.

"Oh, Mr. Pherlon," some of the snottier kids will say when they see him serving cocktails poolside, "bring me a Coke, will ya? Charge it to account number 1376."

This does not bother Mr. Pherlon as much as the kids want it to; some are confused by his polite earnestness when taking their order, and others are impressed at his expert, flat-palmed, above-the-shoulder balance of their tray of soft drinks. As for Monsieur, he is convinced that a waiter, even in America, can have dignity, though he hasn't quite thought out how his work will be valued by those who know nothing about food save how they like their steaks.

The waiter brings him a beer served in a round, stemmed glass manufactured specifically for this brand. What Monsieur likes pointing out to his students is how in France there is nothing wrong with a midmorning beer, how businessmen will come into the cafés for a break and a small, refreshing drink that can take the edge off the morning.

Monsieur himself would enjoy such a tradition at Wilson High, a midmorning beer, a late-afternoon aperitif. He'll ask his students who visit the French schools, "Notice how the teachers all drink wine with their cafeteria lunches?"

Now, a pretty, older woman sits down three tables away from Monsieur. She orders a Dubonnet-blanc and unfolds a *Le Monde*. George Pherlon twitches inside. What a sight, the woman with her ash-blond, styled hair, the soft coral color of her lips and nails, and her smooth, powdered cheeks. She's wearing a spring-blue tailored short skirt and a waist-length jacket, and Mr. Pherlon can hardly stand it. No trips to the Louvre for him this time, no showing fifteen unruly kids a stiff, glassed-in Mona Lisa. It's all here for the looking, the cost of admission only the price of a drink.

The five great women of France, according to Monsieur Pherlon, are Joan of Arc, Eleanor of Aquitaine, Catherine de Médicis, Marie Antoinette (not a great woman, but one of *savoir-vivre* all the same), and Brigitte Bardot.

Every day of Grandes Dames week he tells of a different Dame. From his bulletin board he takes down the "Great Cheeses" pictures from the week before and puts up a collage of museum prints of the regally posed historical women. For Bardot he pins up her last well-known public portrait: a close-up of the star's tanned, somewhat leathery face as she's closing in on middle age. She is hugging a white seal, for it is this picture that marks her retirement from movies and the beginning of the dedication of her life to animal rights.

One day during Grandes Dames week a few years ago a boy brought in an earlier pinup of Brigitte, the famous paparazzi shot of her arching her back as she opens the door of a sportscar outside of the Hôtel Négresco in Nice. There she is, in short-shorts and a bikini top, her 1962 hairstyle with cylinder curls on top and long locks flowing down to her breasts.

"*That's* Brigitte Bardot!" the boy said. "Not the old bag with the seals."

Monsieur Pherlon knew this shot, too. In 1962 he had a desk job in the service as a telephone receptionist at the USO office in Paris. It was a quiet little job. He had pasted this picture on the back inside cover of his office directory. Still, he preferred the later shot—Bardot is exactly his age, and he thought there would be something strange, almost sick, about pinning up a picture of a woman just a couple of years older than his students. Pherlon is a bachelor—but he never liked that word; he was afraid it sounded too swinging or even lecherous for someone in his profession. He likes the sound of the French translation better—*un célibataire*.

For this trip, Monsieur had envisioned spending the mornings in cafés and his afternoons walking around the city and through its parks. He loves his mornings, but yesterday afternoon he began to realize just how much time there is in a day when you don't have fifteen kids to look out for.

The day before, he had found himself reminiscing like a visitor to a city shared with a former lover, only it was his students that the buildings and park benches brought to mind: here's where Barbara Morrison got her hair dyed burgundy; here's where Bobby Martin first discovered steak tartare—the only thing he'd eat for the rest of the trip.

For twenty years Monsieur Pherlon took a group of fifteen students to France for fourteen days in June. They'd stay with families four days in a small, industrial town, then they'd go to Paris, to Provence, and to the Côte d'Azur. Two-thirds of the kids would forget about the trip once they got home; they'd reminisce for a time about that big playground, France. But at least one-third of each group—five people a year—would never be the same.

For twenty years he watched these five kids (usually girls) transform. They'd walk along the streets, looking at business-women dressed in tight skirts with angular sunglasses and all sorts of bangles, earrings, and textured stockings. The young American girls would sit in the metro cars, glancing once or twice at the small dark Frenchmen but unable to keep their eyes off the women, their high heels, their insouciantly tossed scarves. The girls would watch these women for a few days and then Monsieur would find himself negotiating haircuts and permanents at inexpensive salons, leading them to the Galeries Lafayette from where they'd emerge in debt to their fathers' credit cards and having discarded their baggy shorts, tennis shoes, and T-shirts for new miniskirts, ruffly blouses, and colorful sling-back sandals—or whatever came out that year.

It is true that girls develop faster in these matters of culture and style than boys. The boys he would teach the basics, like how to act in a café. If nothing else, they could order *un hot-dog*—a sausage on a baguette smothered with melted Gruyère cheese—and hopefully they would never look at a ballpark frank the same way. The more precocious boys would be shown how to maneuver escargot tongs. Civilized is sexy, girls like it, he might confide to one or two young men once every few years.

The most exciting thing about his evangelism is this: it was never the more popular girls, the pretty, well-dressed, straight-pearly-toothed girls who emerged transformed from the trip. No, it was the pale, stringy-haired girls who had given up at home, but who would now come into their own, finding that style had nothing to do with expensive designer clothes and exacting body proportions.

So what now, Monsieur wonders, looking up and down the street at shopkeepers hosing down the sidewalks. Emptying his beer glass, he feels a sharp pinch of guilt, for it is just a bit too much, France all to himself. He must take it in slowly, not gorging himself all at once: a gourmet, not a gourmand.

He orders another beer. They are, after all, very small portions.

When Monsieur realizes that he is absently staring at that lovely woman across from him, and that she is not so absently looking back, he feigns absorption in his postcard.

But when he looks up again, the woman is still looking at him, squinting the sun out of her amber eyes in a way that draws her lips into a smile. Or maybe she *is* smiling.

Monsieur is not one to flatter himself. True, she has been glancing at him, but her regard is more curious than friendly. Perhaps she wonders about his origins? Though he is obviously an out-of-towner, writing a stack of postcards, Monsieur is rarely tagged for an American right off. Monsieur knows he passes for a Frenchman in all the wrong ways. He's a short man with a round balding head of wiry-black hair. He has the archetypal potbelly, the kind that middle-aged bathers on the Côte d'Azur proudly display, letting it sag over their string mono-kinis.

Not Monsieur. Though he appreciates such a display of well-fed flesh in others, he himself wears a shirt and shorts, sandals and socks to the beach. He brings dark sunglasses and a book. Not to read but to hide behind.

The woman puts her paper on a chair beside her and smooths her skirt over her legs. Monsieur's handwriting becomes illegible. He looks at his watch: an hour until lunch, almost time to menu shop.

He remembers sitting in this café once a few years ago when a group of his students appeared, telling him to come quick, Donny Whitmore was getting thrown into the clink for hurling a wine bottle into the Seine from the Pont Neuf. It seemed that the bottle had hit a tour boat.

The kids had appeared in an anxious flutter, all talking at

once, a few grabbing his arms to rush him along. Monsieur remembers how they trusted him to make things all right, how amazed they seemed at the fluency and ease—a few expertly uttered phrases—with which he convinced the police not to press charges.

Now the memory has a calming effect. In spite of his most willful intentions, Monsieur Pherlon cannot help but reminisce.

His favorite trip was in 1977, the year when the style was crisp blue jeans and leather blazers, when Parisian women wore their hair in one long braid down the middle of their backs. This was the year Sandra Pollard went on the trip, Sandra, who wore her long blond hair braided, after the second day of the trip, down the middle of her back. Sandra had that thick yellow-blond hair that not only turned heads but could cause men and boys to wait outside her hotel just to whistle and clap as she walked by.

Sandra had wanted to go to a discotheque. The entire trip would be a waste, she complained, if she didn't get to go to a real French disco. So when a middle-aged man invited Sandra and her friends to go with him and his friends to a disco, Monsieur allowed it, providing, of course, that he could go along as a chaperon.

"The Black Club" was named solely for its pitch-black darkness inside. The only light came from the glowing dance floor, where Monsieur could see feet dancing, but nothing above the ankles. The squared-off glowing mélange of men's leather shoes and women's high heels and thin ankles was all that was visible in this black club.

A hostess with a pen-sized flashlight led the group to unseen fluffy couches and stuffed chairs. No one saw Monsieur trip and fall over a large coffee table, which he quickly noticed was carpeted; its sharp corners and surface were covered in soft, velvety upholstery.

"Oh, pardon!" Monsieur said as he inadvertently sat down on one of the men.

Soon a waitress brought a bottle of scotch, a bottle of Coca-Cola, a bucket of ice, and glasses. "Mille francs," she asked of the man who had ordered it; two hundred dollars.

Hands met in the dark, fumbling for drinks. A dance song drowned out the giggles and whispers of the girls. Monsieur listened for their voices, wondering in which direction to turn his ear, but all he heard was the music: "Que c'est bon, que c'est bon, que c'est bon quand tu me déshabille." He translated to himself: It's so good, it's so good, it's so good when you take my clothes off. Monsieur strained his ear for voices and worried. He sat there for a while in the darkness, just inches away from men his own age attempting to seduce girls of seventeen.

Thank God he had brought his camera. When a slower, quieter song came on, he pointed the camera in the direction of some silence and flashed a picture, illuminating for a moment a middle-aged man with his hands on the knees of one of Monsieur's wide-eyed, nubile young students. "Oh, hi, Georges," she said, getting up and moving toward him.

The next flash caught Sandra sitting on her date's lap, her arms around his neck. "Georges, you *asshole,*" Sandra said, drunk on straight scotch because the cola had mysteriously disappeared. On the trips he allowed his students to call him by his French name, Georges, but *asshole* was a bit out of line. Still, asshole or not, he knew when joie de vivre might possibly be turning into danger. He snapped another picture, at which Sandra's date growled, "Espèce de con. Merde." One more flash caught Theresa being reluctantly pulled onto a carpeted coffee table by her reclining date. "Oh, there you are, Georges," she said sweetly.

Later, Sandra said to him, "Dance with me, Georges. I don't want to dance with that guy anymore. He's acting really strange."

Monsieur obliged, though he was glad that all anyone could see were his shoes.

46

The evening ended with Monsieur calling a cab and taking the four drunk girls back to the hotel, giggling and laughing about how the men had tried to superglue themselves to the girls on the dance floor, how Georges had rounded them up, secretly, and herded them outside to the waiting cab.

Monsieur had always prided himself on the fact that for twenty years he was able to keep his students out of true danger without depriving them of some fun. But that's not how his superiors saw it last spring. One day in April, Mr. Walker, the school principal, stormed into Monsieur's classroom after school and threw down a small, spiral notebook on Pherlon's desk.

"What's this?" Pherlon asked, leafing through the notebook, but part of him knew. For years George Pherlon had advised his students to write their trip diaries in French. But alas, little Cindy Cooper had written it all down in English.

"Pherlon, is this your idea of a *cultural* exchange trip?"

"I'm not sure what you mean, Mr. Walker."

"Gimme that," Walker said, grabbing the diary out of Pherlon's hand. "Just listen to this, Pherlon:

'June 6th: Georges took us to La Piscine, a club where the dance floor is built inside an old indoor swimming pool. I got really, really, really drunk and danced with some French guy and then kissed around with him *beaucoup*. It was really, really, really fun.

'June 8th: I got drunk again last night and passed out in Bobby Martin's room. He's a jerk. I wish Georges would take us out again where there's some more French guys. The one at La Piscine kept moving up against me when we danced, touching me, like with his arms and his hips. When we sat down he rubbed his feet against my ankles. It was neat. Bobby Martin only uses his hands and he tries for all the same places. Boring.'

"Pherlon, Do you even know what goes on on your trips?"

47

Walker slammed the journal back down on the desk. Monsieur looked through it. There was no mention of the Louvre, no mention of the Opèra, the Eiffel Tower, the Champs Elysées. No, just day after day of entries about drinking champagne and kissing boys.

"Pherlon, have you ever heard of contributing to the delinquency of a minor?"

Monsieur didn't answer; he was engrossed in Cindy's diary. They surprised him so, Cindy's words. He had had her pegged as a whiner. On the trip she had complained that the family she stayed with didn't bathe often enough, they wore the same outfits two days in a row, and ate "cold meatloaf" every night before dinner. (That's pâté, Cindy, Monsieur had had to explain.) So, Cindy Cooper had enjoyed the French after all.

"Did you hear me, Pherlon?"

"I didn't do anything illegal, Mr. Walker. In France, the drinking age is sixteen. Cindy's seventeen. And, when in France—"

"*France!* Forget France, Pherlon. Because here in America, Cindy Cooper's father wants your resignation."

Fortunately, Mr. Cooper was pacified with a formal apology and assurance that George Pherlon would not be chaperoning any more cultural exchanges. Monsieur had tried to salvage his trip, but he soon realized that there was no explaining France to Walker, a man who worked 7 A.M. to 7 P.M. every day and on weekends, a man who ate two school cafeteria lunches daily, and enjoyed them. Walker's decision was final.

Fine, fine, Monsieur had thought then. That's okay. This year I'll have France all to myself.

Through all his recollections, Monsieur forgot that he was staring again, looking dumbly into the face of another. When he finally focuses in on what he had been looking at, the woman in the spring-blue suit appears like a bullet train coming out of a tunnel.

"Bonjour," the woman says in a breezy, singsong tone, but to Monsieur it sounds like an explosion.

"Bonjour," Monsieur answers automatically.

She keeps looking at him with a friendly, but questioning smile.

"Il fait beau, n'est-ce pas?" he says, speaking of the weather.

"Oui." She glances a moment at her empty glass, then looks up again, smiling.

The waiter asks Monsieur if he would like to see a menu. Monsieur gratefully accepts it—for something to do—and begins to look it over.

"It's a nice café for drinks," the woman says, "but the food is not so good." The way she speaks to him in French, Monsieur knows that she does not suspect he is American. "I come here weekdays for my break, but I never lunch here. I don't recommend it."

Ah, yes, lunch, Monsieur thinks. He glances at his watch—it's well past menu-shopping time. "Thank you for the advice," he says to the fine woman, putting the menu aside. He fidgets with his postcards, straightening the pile and putting them into his carry-bag.

"Alors, bonne journée, Madame. Au revoir," he says, nodding, getting up from his chair. He realizes how hasty he must seem, how unfriendly, how maladroit. "À demain pêut-être?" he adds. See you tomorrow?

"À demain," the woman answers, again squinting and smiling her kind but questioning smile.

Monsieur adjusts the strap on his shoulder bag and walks away from the café, thinking, that's plenty. Perhaps he will come here tomorrow, continue this acquaintance, gradually getting to know this gracious woman on her coffee break until one day maybe they will lunch together. It's a thought—he has twenty-seven more days, after all. Twenty-seven more

49

days. All to himself.

But he tries not to think about that now. He quickens his steps, but before he can turn the corner out of her sight, he hears someone call after him

"Monsieur. Eh—Monsieur!" The waiter is following him, holding up Monsieur's little unpaid ticket. With his round tray under one arm, he runs with heavy but efficient steps, as if catching tourists who dine and dash were the bulk of his occupation.

"Oh, pardon," Monsieur says, adding in French, "you see, I forgot. I am late, you understand—"

"Américain?" the waiter asks.

"Oui," Monsieur admits. He glances over at the woman, who is refolding her newspaper, subtly glancing at his little fiasco.

"It is the Americans who always forget to pay," the waiter says. While Monsieur fumbles with the money in his money belt, the waiter stands, puffed up like a saluting soldier, his tray under his arm.

"Combien?" Monsieur asks. How much?

"Zirty-zix and zixty," the waiter says in exasperated English. Pherlon hands the waiter a fifty-franc note. The waiter pulls out his leather coin purse for change, but Monsieur motions refusal.

"Service is included," the waiter snaps.

Monsieur knows service is included. For twenty years he told his students that service is included unless the menu specifically states, "Service non-compris."

He begins to insist, but it's no use. The waiter will take no bribe. Monsieur puts the heavy coins in his pocket; they jingle loudly there as he walks away. Before he turns the corner, Monsieur glances back toward the terrasse, now empty of customers.

It is with shaky, anxious steps that Monsieur jumps on the

first arriving train in the subway station. Never, in all his years, has a waiter refused a side tip. It has been at least fifteen years since a Frenchman has spoken English to Monsieur, for Monsieur had always eased through France so expertly, even when leading his gaggle of noisy, awkward students.

Monsieur has never really been bothered by that old saying, "Those who can't, teach," for it never really applied to him. Monsieur knows French and he knows France. But he often wonders about those other teachers, the art and music teachers, the coaches, those who year after year watch the young students surpass their own mediocrity.

"It is enough just to recognize and nurture the possibilities," Mr. Davis, the band teacher, once said in the smoky teachers' lounge. Far from being jealous of his students with superior talent, Davis has a whole wall of the band room plastered with framed articles about those who went on to achieve some success in the music world beyond the realm of the marching band.

And then there were the coaches, long past their prime, who used their offices for nothing but to display the well-polished trophies of their winning sports stars.

Pherlon has no trophies; his students have rarely placed in the state academic merit awards in French. But he has a drawer full of postcards from students who return to France years after their trip with Monsieur. "Cher Georges," they will write. "Me voilà à Paris et je pense à toi." Here I am in Paris, and I'm thinking of you.

Sitting by himself in the quiet metro car under the streets of Paris, Monsieur Pherlon knows that postcards like these will soon become rarer and rarer; soon even the swishy rumors of his trips will have faded from the consciousness of the student body that gets younger and cleaner-cut, more ambitious and more foreign to him every year. Soon, perhaps, they will start to win more academic merit awards in French.

51

What's worse, he thinks, is this: it's being alone in Paris where the only one I have to keep from looking like an ass is myself.

He sits in the yellow-and-blue car that seems to float on its rubber wheels. Before the doors snap shut, there is a long, reedy tone that sounds like an organ note. To some, this warning signal might sound like an irritating, grinding noise, but because of Penny Van Meter, it sounds like music to Monsieur.

He remembers when Penny came into his classroom once after school with her clarinet. Penny had gone on his trip the summer before.

"Guess what this is, Monsieur Pherlon," she said. She blew a long thin note.

"I couldn't tell you," he said, thinking, a middle C perhaps?

"It's the warning signal they sound before they shut the doors on the Paris metro. Listen."

And indeed it was, just the exact thin, reedy tone, or at least a perfect memory of it. She left the room giggling, as Monsieur counted the months until his trip, looking outside at the conveyer-belt flow of boxy cars lumbering through town on the crowded gray freeway.

Monsieur gets off at Châtelet-Les Halles. As he walks by the ticket booth he sees two women with a phrase book, trying to ask instructions while a line of impatient French commuters shout near obscenities at them. The man in the booth shrugs his shoulders and waves them away. The women huddle together, crushed and afraid, too lost to be humiliated.

Monsieur has this theory: if you don't go to Paris by the time you're twenty-five you might as well not go at all. After twenty-five, it's too late. He looks over at the two lost women and he's sorry for them. France to you, he thinks, will always mean thick muddy coffee that tastes burned, noisy, rude people who don't bathe every day and who cut in line, hotel rooms without private toilets.

Still, he must do what he can.

"Where are you trying to go?" Monsieur asks them. The frustration clears from their faces; they look younger than he had thought.

"Oh," the tall one says, "someone who speaks *English*. Thank God!"

"We've been trying to get to the Eiffel Tower for two hours, but we keep getting lost," the other one says. "I wish we were in England, where they speak the language."

No, Monsieur thinks. You cannot wish you were in England. Monsieur hasn't been to England for twenty-three years. He has vague memories of rain, pubs that didn't stay open late enough, and pureed canned peas. He has never seen the attraction to a country that has some sappy nostalgia for the postwar age of austerity and all that stiff-upper-lip stuff.

"Have you been to the Galeries Lafayette?" he asks them. "It's much more interesting than the Eiffel Tower. And the Eiffel Tower is much nicer if you admire it from this café just off the Champs du Mars. He does not tell them what he knows, that the Eiffel Tower won't be nearly as interesting to them as the men and women walking down the busy sidewalk, all of them looking like they're going someplace secret and otherworldly. He takes out his street map and draws directions. "Order a Lillet to drink," he adds, spelling it out for them, knowing that this light, sweet aperitif will suit these beginners well.

"And you might like to dine at this place, the Restaurant Chartier," he adds. "And this dance club, La Piscine." He circles the block on the map; he tells them how much to tip the doorman.

"Take this, too," he says, giving them his pocket-sized metro map that he knows by heart. "Here comes your train. Change at Concorde."

The girls walk forward, reluctantly, then glance a moment back at him. He knows they're trying to figure out whether or not he should be trusted. Finally, they do as he says.

Though they themselves may be a bit unsure, Monsieur is quite sure that if they dine at Restaurant Chartier and dance at La Piscine, they have a one-in-three chance of changing their lives forever.

He also knows that there are countless too many students wandering around Paris this summer, wishing they were in England, where people speak the language.

The girls sit by the window, looking into the map as if it will lead to a buried treasure. Monsieur watches the train pull away until it disappears into a tunnel.

Momentarily, another train floats into the station with a rubber-wheeled *whoosh*. Its doors snap open, and a crowd of colorfully dressed commuters pours out. Monsieur is overtaken, for a moment, by the sounds of throaty, run-together words, of ladies' heels clicking across the tiled platform, of the thin, reedy warning tone, and the snap of the closing doors.

He thinks of those girls arriving soon at the Café du Coin. A dreamy, exhausted feeling like jet lag rushes over him, but with all the exhilaration of being someplace new. For a moment Monsieur considers going back to his hotel for a little rest, but there's still so much more to do today. There's lunch, of course, but after that he has a busy afternoon ahead of him.

It will take some time, he knows, to become an expert on where young tourists are most likely to get lost. But for now, he gets on the next train—any direction will do—and looks for the next lost young American who needs just a little instruction.

OTT'S TORNADO, 1931

MAY
Our bad luck can't last forever, Edna says to her husband, Ott, as she goes through the wallpaper samples sent from the hardware store. How's this? she says, taping up samples over the dull gray plaster on the living room wall, rebuilt after last summer's tornado. Edna takes her time lingering over the choices; she likes the flower designs best. Finally she orders, on credit, the paper with the bright red poppies set against a white blue like the summer's clear sky.

JUNE
They say the paste on Edna's wallpaper wasn't even dry when the next tornado hit. With this one, Edna and Ott lost everything—what the wind didn't take, a hailstorm ruined.

For the time being they settle into a rented house in town. "It's nice for a change," Edna says to the well-wishers dropping by. She talks of the new house they'll build next year.

JULY
Ott comes home with the bill for the wallpaper from the hardware store. "Sixty days past due," it says, rubber-stamped in red.

"Don't they know about our tornado?" Edna asks.

"Haven't they heard about our bad luck?"

Edna and Ott never did get out of debt enough to buy their own home again, and little by little they lost their farm. Some say it's because they started off with a bad piece of land; others say that with two tornadoes, it was just plain bad luck. Some say it was because Edna got so sick during the depression; others say they just gave up.

Ott never talked much about his tornadoes. But if you mentioned them to Edna, she'd tell of how the second one hit just after they had hung her new wallpaper with the bright red flowers. She'd go on to tell of the bill from the hardware store, then she'd stop, sit back, and just see if you'd ask that question that's been with her all those years: "When you lost everything like that, wouldn't you think they'd just forget about the bill for the wallpaper?"

THE DINING ROOM CAPTAIN

My first job out of college was waitressing at a country club, and by now the idea of a college graduate waiting tables should surprise no one, though at the time, I was surprised and, I suppose, a little sad, for I was first-generation college, and I remember my father saying to me when I showed him my diploma, "See that, Rita? No one can take that way from you." Indeed, no one took it away from me, but nonetheless it seemed to lose something, hanging on the girlish pink walls of my bedroom in my parents' house, where I was living in hopes of saving money to pay off college debts while working at the country club and sending out résumés.

You might say that I planned rather poorly, majoring in French literature, and you'd be right. I wasn't really learning any job skills, though as it turned out, I was hired over ten other college graduates because I could pronounce the dishes, the wines, the liqueurs of fine dining.

I was hardly one of those clever and wise, happy-with-their-lot sort of waitresses that you sometimes read about or see in the movies, yet I didn't entirely hate my job, either. It was, for the most part, a lousy and low-paying job, but it did have its moments.

Like getting ready for work. I liked that. I'd spend the

morning sending out letters and résumés and making phone calls, enthusiastically, at first, but after a year, less so. In the afternoons, I'd borrow the pool of a nearby apartment complex. Then at about four I took a shower, arranged my hair into a sleek chignon and splashed this citrusy after-shower cologne all over myself, topping it off with a cool dusting of powder and slipping my smooth black-and-white uniform over it all.

Before leaving my parents' house I poured myself a large glass of iced tea for the drive to work. I put it in a real glass— a glass glass, not paper or plastic or Styrofoam, because it made driving through town, through that jungle of Hardee's and gas stations and strip malls, to a lousy job a little easier to take. I liked the sound of the ice cubes clinking against the glass that I held between my legs to cool me as I drove in my unair-conditioned Rabbit.

That summer was so hot and humid that I never put my stockings on until I got into the air-conditioned club. The female employees' bathroom was always smoky and crowded, the yellow cinderblock walls sticky in the unventilated heat. All the waitresses maneuvered for a space in front of the one tiny mirror above the one sink, but me, I'd steal away to the members' bathroom, which was usually deserted in the late afternoon. I'd take my time in the cool, spacious carpeted room, sitting at the well-lit dressing tables in front of the mirrors that spanned the length and width of the walls, helping myself to the free lotions and hairsprays, finishing my makeup and then just sitting there, spacing out, really, until it was time to clock in. I liked that.

And I liked an old waitress named Cassie, whose secret to being the most requested and heavily tipped waitress was to treat the members as if they were very, very ill. "In a way, you're like a social worker," she told me once when a member named Mr. Hammond threw a tantrum because I forgot that he simply could not bear chives on his sour cream. "This isn't a club, it's an asylum, and the pour soul is crazy." She leaned into me and added, "Because you'd have to be crazy to pay what it costs to belong here!"

It worked for Cassie; she didn't seem to mind her position. She doted over the members as charitably as an old nurse with a sick child. But me—while I didn't particularly *like* the members, I couldn't quite see them as crazy. Crazy people, it would seem, would be somewhat unpredictable, and after a few months of working there, I knew who wanted what when, down to the quarter teaspoon of pickled onion juice in Mr. Barton's Gibson.

Most of all, I guess, I liked Paul. He, like me, had recently graduated from college—a business major—and unlike me, he had faith. He was sure that everything would work out and that sometime, not so very far off, he'd be walking into the front door of the country club, not through the employees' entrance through the loading dock. He was sure of it, and mostly I envied him his optimism. Still, I had been out of college a year, he only a few months.

A stocky, muscular man with curly black hair and dark brown eyes, he looked swell in his white ruffly shirt and vest. Other waiters would complain that the shirts made them look effeminate (though they didn't use that term), but the blousy shirt was no threat to Paul; he looked more like a bullfighter than a waiter.

Paul was a little older than me—maybe twenty-five or twenty-six—for he had taken a few years off in college to surf in southern California, where he had finagled a job selling time-share condos for a local firm, convincing his boss that the best way to make contacts would be mingling on the most exclusive beaches. That was Paul.

Sometimes we'd go for a drink after work. "Want to go 'across the street'?" he'd ask, though it was actually almost a mile, across the freeway, to the Ramada Inn Lounge. It was there that he would tell me of his plans, how he'd taken a club directory home and memorized the names and companies and positions of the most important members, how he was waiting for the right moment to make contacts, here and there. I'd listen to him. I admired his guile and his earnestness, and I'd wonder why I couldn't do the same thing myself. Often we'd dance to the live music, an electric keyboard/drum machine singing duo, and later we'd end up, like high school students without a better place to go (he, too, lived at home), in the backseat of my Volkswagen Rabbit.

One day Paul asked me to make a tape of the correct pronunciations of the wines we served at the club. As I made the tape, I pictured him driving to work in the mornings, wearing his fluffy waiter's shirt, repeating after me: *Veuve Clicquot, Louis Jadot, Château Moreau.*

A month later he was promoted to dining room captain.

By then it was August, and besides a new job, Paul also had a fiancée, a finance something-or-other by day who'd whisk him away every night after work at eleven on the dot. Our late-night hotel bar dancing was over, though sometimes when we were both scheduled for the lunch and dinner split shifts we'd steal away during our two-hour breaks, going back to his parents' house while they were at work. Paul would practice his tableside cooking techniques, making for me all the elegant dishes we served at the club: hot spinach salad and shrimp Sir Edward, Steaks de Burgo and Dianne, which we'd complement with wine salvaged from the half-finished bottles of noontime business luncheons. He'd throw his head back and laugh crazily as he made the flames tease the ceiling, where he'd unplugged the smoke detector weeks before.

And sometimes in the middle of the hot afternoons when all but the un- or underemployed were at their office jobs, Paul and I made love. It was on those days, driving back to our shifts in the burning late afternoon, that I liked it right where I was, sitting next to him in a hot car, wearing my short, smooth, black-and-white uniform, checking my lipstick in the rearview mirror, holding a cool glass of iced coffee between my knees as I pinned back my hair. Zipping through town with Paul on those afternoons, I could forget where I was headed; Paul made me feel that good.

But then we'd get back to work and I'd watch him craft the flames of his desserts as he had for me, but now it was for the members, who would *oooh* and *ahhh* and with whom he would chat so naturally that it wasn't long before I saw it: one of the better-connected members handing Paul a business card as Paul helped the man's wife on with her coat.

And then at night Paul would kiss me lightly in the darkened dining room before he went out to the loading dock where his fiancée was waiting in her car. Me, I'd go out with the cooks and the dishwashers and watch the day's sports highlights at the bar across the freeway, drinking a Bud, thinking about how much I loved to watch Paul dressing in front of his mirror, how he'd do and redo his bow tie (no clip-on for Paul!) until it was just right. I'd linger lazily on the bed, watching him, sometimes trying to catch his eye in the mirror, distract him for just one second, but Paul, whatever he did, he did well.

I had never seen a Filofax until Paul brought his to work and showed it to me. It was intricate, with the calendar and phone numbers and scratch pads and maps and Zip Code charts and a place for all the business cards he was collecting. He showed me his three-month plan—he was going to have a job in three months, a *real* job. His tasks and goals were marked and highlighted in different colors. He had a complicated but clear system for when he would send his résumés, make his follow-up calls, get the interviews, and write the thank-you letters and then when he'd start the cycle again.

"And here," he said, pointing to a Saturday in spring, "here's the day I'm getting married."

He never quite said we had to knock it off, but I knew it was over one afternoon when we both worked the split shift. I was setting the last table after lunch and he came to me and said, "Not today. I'm going to the library to do some research."

And at that moment I felt an odd relief, a splendid happiness, for finally, I too had a goal: I wanted him back.

One night in late August, we were way overstocked in bananas, and the club manager was offering a fifty-cent bonus for every Bananas Foster Flambé we could sell.

Me, I couldn't sell ice water in the Sahara. Oh, I'd lamely try but when I'd say something like, "May I suggest the Bananas Foster Flambé for dessert?" the members would suddenly look at me, startled as if seeing me for the first time all evening, thinking, "Who are *you*?" But here was Paul, chatting up the members, saying, "May I suggest the Bananas Foster? It's my personal favorite, and we leave all the calories in the kitchen." I've heard that "calories in the kitchen" line at every restaurant I've ever worked at, but Paul, he'd smile, the ladies would giggle, and by God, they'd buy it! They'd buy whatever he was selling, and that night, even the chintzy Cheneys ordered the Bananas Foster for their entire party of twelve.

By now Paul and I had our tableside presentation perfectly timed. I would appear with the finely rounded scoops of ice cream in crystal dishes on a white doilied tray and join Paul's side just as he set the bananas on fire, shaking the pan until the flames almost reached the ceiling and then gently died down at his command. I'd stand there, tray in hands, like a magician's assistant who has seen the trick a thousand times but still believes in the magic.

For the Cheneys' group of twelve, Paul needed two pans, two burners. He stood, twirling the pans in the air by their handles, holding the attention of all in the party, if not in the club. As he melted the sugar and the butter, he answered culinary questions from the gushing and admiring wives, at one point asking them to please close their eyes—he had a secret ingredient he wished to add. (A pinch of salt!) They did as they were told. Just before his finale—the lighting of two pans at once—he took off his jacket, as if to say, "Nothing up my sleeve!"

And then, in an uncharacteristically clumsy split second of his life, he turned, knocking over a half-empty short glass from the busboy's stand. He caught it in an elegant maneuver, though upside down, before it reached the carpet. It was then I saw it there on the floor, the little plastic sword with three tiny pickled onions, and I realized that what was spilled on Paul's sleeve was the remains of Mr. Barton's half-finished Gibson.

I leaned over to pick up the tiny sword just as Paul was tilting the pans into the flames. "No—" I said, but it was a split second after, not before, he set the Bananas Foster aflame, along with his billowy sleeve.

I was told that what I did was heroic and quick thinking, if not a little sloppy. I snapped the tablecloth off the Hammonds' nearby table, flinging the silverware, china, glassware, and Caesar salads dramatically across the room. As much as I'm not crazy about the idea of Paul going up in flames, I did not mind a Caesar salad landing in Mrs. Hammond's lap. It was all quite a spectacle, I was told, as the busboy poured his bucket of melting ice over Paul and the flaming cart and I wrapped Paul in the tablecloth, hugging him until the flames died out. Longer.

"If you will excuse me," Paul said to the guests. I swear he bowed, but others said he was doubling over from the pain; his walk to the kitchen was as dignified and steady as a soldier's. Once inside, he fainted.

"I'm finished, you know," Paul said from his hospital bed.

"Don't be silly," I answered.

"No," he said. "I crashed and burned, didn't I? In front of the Cheneys and the Hammonds. And were the Bollmans still there? The Lawtons, had they left? Who else saw? I must have looked like such a fool. When did I faint?"

Paul got worker's comp for two weeks and at first he didn't like it, getting a paycheck for nothing. "It's a bad habit," he said.

"It gives you time to work on your three-month plan," I said.

"Three-month plans don't work," he answered. He looked pale and exhausted; the glimmer had gone out of his eyes. "You never know what will happen."

One day in late September, a few weeks after Paul came back to work, I was killing time between my split shifts, sitting outside dangling my legs over the loading dock, catching the last rays of the warmish sunlight, looking out at the golf course's billowy trees beyond the drained pool; thinking how it still felt funny, unreal, how, unlike school, the working life wasn't tied to any seasons at all; that here it was, almost fall, and nothing was changing except the weather.

Paul walked out of the back door, car keys clanging and catching the sunlight in one hand, his other hand outstretched toward me. "C'mon," he said. "I've been thinking."

He unbuttoned the top two buttons of his collar as he drove; his bow tie hung vertically down his shirt.

"I give up. I'm through with this three-month-plan stuff." He explained that the interviews he'd missed weren't being so easily rescheduled.

"What else are you going to do?" I said.

"Be a damned good dining room captain," he said. "The best dining room captain in Des Moines. That should be enough."

He took a pack of imported cigarettes out of his jacket pocket. "The Johnstones at table eight left these," he said, lighting one. We all had an impressive collection of snooty

64

cigarettes left behind by drunken members. "The work isn't so lousy," he went on. "I even kind of like the showing-off, the *cha-cha-cha* of it. It suits me and the time goes by like *that*." He snapped his silver lighter shut. "And there are perks. Like free cigarettes."

"Will that be enough for you?" I said.

"It's got to be," he answered. " 'Cause I'm just sick of wanting something else."

I wondered if you could really help it, what you wanted.

I should have been thrilled to be with him once again in his room, and as he undressed me he said that it didn't have to be the afternoons anymore, that maybe his being engaged to someone else wasn't such a good idea.

But my mind wasn't so much on us. I was thinking about how his room was kind of a mess right now, and for the first time ever he had left his closet door half-open. On the top shelf there was a gray-and-green painted model airplane he had most likely built years ago, during that time before boys get interested in girls, careers. I was surprised that he had not yet thrown it away.

I used to have this conjecture about death. Death would be whatever you believed it would be. If you thought it was nothing at all, then when you died you would simply cease to be. If you believed, as you lay dying, that there was a heaven and that you deserved it, well, then, by God, to heaven you'd go (even if you'd been a creep here on earth—all that counted was your belief). Likewise about hell, or whatever else you believed. Perhaps in death you thought you'd get to meet a dead rock star or Marie Antoinette, if you wanted to. Maybe you'd get to float around the living like a fly on the wall and find out how everyone really lived. Maybe you relived and refelt again and again your life's best moments or favorite places: a placid Minnesota lake in summer or a desert landscape by an ocean. The important thing—and here's the catch—was that you had to believe in *something* (even if it was in the nothingness) and that your vision of death had to be clear and uncomplicated and wholly believed or you'd have to muck around for the rest of eternity, befuddled and lost, watching everyone else end up however it was they had believed they would. It was not a question of believing in the one true and good thing, but believing with all your soul in something. You couldn't think, "Well, maybe," and just hope for the best, and even being good wasn't enough. That was my vision of death.

But that summer, I began to think that that scenario had more to do with life.

I had not yet found the thing for which I'd light myself on fire; it was not (and would never be) as clearly envisioned as walking through the front doors of a country club. Still, whatever that thing was I sought, I knew that it had nothing to do with helping a young man lose sight of his dreams.

"Rita," he said, dressing before the mirror that last afternoon we were together. "I'm glad that it was you who was standing next to me when I caught on fire. It could have been so much worse."

I went over and ran my fingers lightly along the tender pink flesh on his arm. "But just think how much better it would have been," I said, "had it been me going up in flames. You could have saved me."

He looked at me thoughtfully, urging me on, as if imagining the reversal for the first time.

"Had it been me on fire," I said, "you'd have reacted much, much quicker. You'd have made it into an event! Oh, the members—they wouldn't have been screaming, they'd have been applauding, and you—you would have even saved the Bananas Foster!"

I stood there, watching him smile slightly into the mirror as he did his black bow tie, hastily looping the ends around and pulling them through. He started to straighten it but then he caught my eye and he turned, taking his hands from his tie and placing them on my hips, drawing me toward him.

I leaned away, looking at him critically. "Your tie—it's crooked," I said, waiting.

Relieved, he turned into the mirror and fussed with it until it was perfect.

JESSIE, OCTOBER 1, 1933

Jessie—Grandmother would say her name in a whisper and a hiss. Jessie was married to Grandma's brother, and it was because Jessie was on his mind that day that he got himself killed. What else would distract him so? Why else would he pull his maintainer onto the tracks in the path of the train? It had to be Jessie he was thinking of, his troubles with Jessie, for everyone knew what Jessie'd been up to.

That's about all anyone ever had to say about Jessie, except for Aunt Sally, who would sometimes dreamily say, "Sure, I remember Jessie—she had those red, red lips and wore those white high heels . . ." Depending on whom you talked to, Jessie was either a would-be screen star displaced on a forty-acre farm or something else entirely.

On the dusty floorboards of Grandma's attic, I once found a picture of a stout, plain woman standing on a dingy front porch. On the back of the photo someone had written, "Jessie, October 1, 1933." She did not look like the woman who could make Grandma hiss and Aunt Sally smile. Not until you looked closer and thought of what they'd said about her could you see it, how she was standing in a sheer, sleeveless dress, as if it wasn't October, wearing white high-heeled pumps, as if she wasn't miles from anywhere she could kick up her heels. She had her hair in the style of a flapper's permanent wave; she was standing erect and dignified like a cover girl for *American Woman,* as if the porch she was standing on was not caked with the dust that had blown through from the Great Plains, as if her husband's crops had not burned out that year, as if the boards underneath her pretty shoes were not rotting.

Jessie does not smile. It's as if she's challenging her sister-in-law, and all those who will look at her picture over the years, to go ahead and think what they will of her, whose husband will soon be killed on the tracks, who would ditch the failing farm, take the insurance money, and get on a train to California, wearing white high-heeled shoes and a sheer, sleeveless dress, never to be seen around this dirty old farm again.

DRESSING IT UP

Frannie orders a whiskey sour, imagining an amber-colored cocktail in a small tulip glass with a blurry cherry among the sparkling ice cubes. But her drink doesn't come in a dainty cocktail glass. No, what Frannie gets is a huge blistered-glass tumbler with melting crushed ice, too much whiskey, syrupy sour mix, and a plastic sword that spears three cherries and an orange slice. She should have expected this much.

It's still light outside, this early spring day. The Holiday Inn bar has floor-to-ceiling windows that look south, behind the hotel. There's a hill, a brown bank, a steel fence, and some sky, but it's all they could do with what they had, Frannie thinks. This view is better than what's on the other side of the building—the Brooklyn-Queens Expressway and La Guardia airport.

A few businessmen come in to the bar and ask the bartender if it's happy hour. Frannie knows the men are here at happy hour just by chance, for surely no one planned to get here at five-thirty on purpose to have syrupy drinks. Frannie is the only one in this bar who is not imminently on her way elsewhere; she will be staying a while. A grinning middle-aged man furtively looks around the room while taking off his overcoat and draping it over the bar. He orders a drink, then he looks at Frannie, and in spite of herself, Frannie keeps look-ing at him, but only to see if he's still looking at her, and of course, he is. She tries to muster an "I'm here on business" look, but she knows she's not fooling anyone. She's too young to be important enough to fly anywhere on business. Her short suit is more cute than businesslike, which, she now realizes, is why she chose it.

Her mistake was to be here on time. Here's how it should have happened: Maurice should be sitting where she is now, ordering his second drink, wondering if Frannie would come. Then Frannie would have walked in. She'd sit down next to him on this mauve upholstered bench seat, and with a down-ward glance she'd squeeze the hand that had gently taken hers under the table. Something like that.

And now she makes another mistake. She glances toward the door, once again catching the eye of the man at the bar. He nods; she looks away. "Goddammit," Frannie thinks, not so much dreading getting rid of him, but dreading the chitchat beforehand. Where ya headed? What d'ya do? And worse yet, Where are you from?

"You've got to say it like it's someplace special," her friend Viv had told her. "When people ask you where you're from, pretend you're going to say, 'I'm from Brazil,' but when you get to the Brazil part, substitute Nebraska."

They were in a SoHo wine bar with track lighting that beamed down to backlight the customers, no matter where they sat. A German photojournalist had just politely excused himself, not coincidentally, Viv maintained, after Frannie had told him what she did and where she was from.

"Why do you have to say it like that?" Viv asked. "And why can't you tell people you do something else besides work as a secretary?"

"Next time I'll tell them I'm a ballerina."

"No, you don't have to lie," Viv said. "Just dress it up."

Viv is a clerk at Madelon D'Arcy's, an exclusive hat shop in SoHo. She also helps to sew the hats, and sometimes she'll arrange a hatband or a flower in a different manner than Madelon's patterns call for. So Viv is able, without really lying, to tell people that she designs hats. Viv's from Minnesota, and when she tells people this, she lowers her voice and looks them in the eye like she's letting them in on a big secret.

Frannie's job is a little harder to dress up. Secretary. She could say, bilingual secretary at a French import-export firm, but they'd still ask her what she does and she'd say type and file and answer the phone.

Viv prodded her: "Is there anything about your job that you *like*?"

"I like Maurice," Frannie had said.

"Obviously," Viv answered. "But what else?"

Frannie thought for a while, taking a sip from her wine, for while the wine bar served a hundred wines by the glass, they did not serve cocktails. "Okay," Frannie finally said. "How's this: I like walking from the subway stop from Lexington to Fifth Avenue and up a few blocks to Rockefeller Center on my way to work, past Saks, and the bookstores and shoe shops. And there's this little candy shop that has wonderful displays in the window, with colored cellophane wrapping and confetti that make the boxes of candy sparkle like jewelry. I like that."

"Yeah, what else?"

"I like getting a cappuccino and a croissant at this coffee shop in the lobby of my building, and since I'm always early I take it upstairs and sit at Maurice's big oak desk by the window, and I look at all the people going up and down the avenue into work, into the skyscrapers that look like huge boxes of candy."

Viv rolled her eyes, downed the last half-sip of her drink. "What do you do then? At work?"

"I go back to my desk and see what's been dumped into my in-tray."

"C'mon, what else do you like?" Viv asked. "Besides Maurice, besides Fifth Avenue coffee shops and chocolate-box buildings?"

"What else is there to like?" Frannie asked, but Viv was distracted by a young woman walking by in a foam-green, black-feathered beret. "Not one of Madelon's," Viv muttered.

Frannie tried to think of other things that she liked. She had moved to New York after completing only two years of college at the University of Colorado, where she had taken a few core courses in geology and some advanced French literature courses. When she ran out of money for school, she decided to work for a while, and she looked for a city where she wouldn't have to wait tables and where she didn't need a car. She ended up in New York. When she got her job as a bilingual secretary, she thought she was doing pretty well for someone with little work experience and no college degree. But then she noted that when people asked her what she did, and she told them, the response was almost always, "Oh, and you *like* that?"

She knew her job was nothing special as far as work went. It was work. New York, it's the only place she'd ever lived where so many people seemed to love their jobs. In Colorado, people worked so that they could ski. And in Nebraska, work was just work, unadorned. But now, in New York City, Frannie notices that people chant, "I love my job," like people in airports chant "Hare Krishna."

"Sometimes I translate," Frannie told Viv. "About once a week a letter comes in, in French, and I write up a translation of it to go in the file."

"There you go! So next time tell them you're a translator," Viv said.

Frannie looked at her friend the hat designer. She was wearing a black lace fedora with a barely yellow satin rose on the side. It would have cost $350 had Viv not just borrowed it from the shop for the night. "We can't go anywhere we might see Madelon," she had said.

Frannie would not, of course, tell the man at the bar that she was a translator. She would not lean into him and whisper, "Nebraska." If he did come over, this man wouldn't care what she said besides yes or no to "Can I buy you a drink?" And for now, he won't even have the chance to do this because he is looking toward a tall flight attendant with a chin-length blunt cut of thick black hair who is standing at the other end of the brass-and-wood bar.

The ice has melted in her half-empty whiskey sour. She would like to order another drink, but one that isn't so horsey. She decides that she will order her next drink straight up, for surely then it will be served in a real cocktail glass.

The tumblers at the bar rattle from a jet flying low overhead. A pilot comes in and talks to the flight attendant at the bar. He is a tall, older man with a freshly shaven face and a full head of smooth, graying hair, and the flight attendant is delighted to see him. Frannie imagines them necking on the airplane before the other crew members and passengers arrive.

And then it occurs to her that maybe the woman is not a flight attendant, but a pilot. She can't tell by the uniform. Frannie has never seen a female commercial airpilot. They must exist, just like male flight attendants, but she hasn't seen any. Frannie wonders whether, at twenty-two, she is too old to become a pilot. She doesn't really want to, but she'd hate to think it was too late.

Frannie remembers finding her mother's pilot's license in a desk drawer. "Back then," her mother explained, "some people thought having your own airplane would be as common as having your own car. So during the fifties, a lot of us learned to fly."

"Why didn't you keep it up, as a hobby?" Frannie had asked.

"It wasn't as much fun as they said it would be. I remember how the other women would tell me to go up in the afternoon when the sun was shimmering over the fields. They'd say there was nothing like it, flying solo. But I'd be up there looking out over the fields, and about four o'clock I'd start thinking, 'It's happy hour at the bar at the Hotel Berlingmar. What am I doing up here all by myself?' "

Frannie knows the bar at the Hotel Berlingmar. While boys have bought her drinks and reached for her under the table, she has sat in the booths and looked at the black-and-white photos on the walls of the bar's glory days: smoky blurs of servicemen dipping and twirling their dance partners; more young men in uniform at the bar with their arms around their buddies, smiling glassy-eyed into the camera as if they weren't being shipped off the next day; a waitress arching her back and tilting her head, flashing a toothy smile as she balances a half-dozen beers on a small round tray, beers served in V-shaped pilsner glasses.

Now the bar at the Hotel Berlingmar no longer has a dance floor, and the leather upholstery in the booths is patched and frayed. It is frequented mostly by transients who sit at the bar and watch the television overhead, or frat boys who come downtown to slum it.

Still, it's a place where highballs are served in highball glasses, this last old hotel bar in Grand Island.

The Holiday Inn bar across from La Guardia is packed with people dressed, like Frannie, from their day at work. Almost everyone except Frannie has a briefcase and carry-on luggage, containing most likely a change of clothes or a fresh shirt, a shaving or cosmetic kit, reports and proposals.

Frannie smoothes her short skirt over her stockings. The stockings are top-of-the-line *Tcha!,* an expensive brand her firm imports. They were a gift from Genevieve, one of the account executives, and they really are nice stockings. She had saved them for a special occasion, and today, when she put them on they were so silky they felt like butter in her hands.

Since the firm has acquired the *Tcha!* account, *Tcha!* has become a buzzword in the office. People will say, "Ooh, how *Tcha!*" at someone's new outfit or haircut. It can refer to the acquisition of a particularly juicy account, or even a party given by one of the account executives. Maurice had referred to Frannie as being "très *Tcha!*" once when she had found a file that had been missing for weeks.

Not long ago, a brown-paper parcel came for Maurice. As the rest of the employees gathered around, he opened up the gift, which was from the *Tcha!* firm in France. It was an enlarged, framed ad for *Tcha!* as it appeared in French fashion magazines, picturing a pair of long, smooth legs crossed beneath a café table, with a shoeless foot caressing a man's ankle. The caption read, "*Tcha! C'est Toi!*" Frannie has seen the same ad in American magazines. It reads, "*Tcha!* It's You!"

Frannie confided to Genevieve that she thought it was crazy for someone to pay fifteen dollars for even the least expensive of the *Tcha!* line.

"Why?" Genevieve had said. "Fifteen dollars isn't too much to spend to feel, well, *Tcha!* And what's wrong with feeling *Tcha!?*"

Genevieve is the senior account executive; she has smooth, ash-blond hair, pearly blue eyes, all the grace and sophistication of well-bred middle age, as well as a distinct brand of Euro-American savoir faire, the intricacies of which she's often eager to share with Frannie.

Genevieve had once tried to get the others at the office to call Frannie by her full name, Francine. "It's such a *Midwestern* habit to shorten names," she had said. "Besides, are you sure you're not a Francine?"

"Take my word for it. I'm a Frannie," Frannie had said.

Though she had tried, Genevieve could not make the name stick. She conceded one day, saying, "*Frannie*. That's really sort of cute. It's like what you'd call a *gamine,* one of those clever young girls with thick-cropped, boyish haircuts. Like Jean Seberg in *Breathless*. It fits."

In spite of herself, Frannie had liked the comparison.

Frannie was also grateful for the stockings, though she wondered if they would have the same effect on her as they did on Genevieve. Frannie had no doubt that in the mornings, after showering and dusting herself with some perfume-counter talc from Bergdorf's, Genevieve would pull on a pair of silky *Tcha!* stockings, never snagging them with her smooth, painted fingernails. She'd check her lipstick in the mirror and walk out of her apartment, saying good morning to the doorman, and then walk five blocks to their office at Rockefeller Center.

Genevieve often gave Frannie clever little gifts, like *Tcha!* stockings, lipsticks, and candy, sometimes for staying late to retype a marketing proposal, but often for nothing at all. Once she gave Frannie a desk calendar of American paintings in the Museum of Modern Art. Every week Frannie would turn over the page to a new painting, and beside each masterpiece she would scribble her week's deadlines. For Christmas, she gave Frannie a membership to the museum, only a five-block walk from their office.

One late winter afternoon, Genevieve pulled Frannie from the windowless secretarial pool into her office, and told her to look outside.

"See that?" Genevieve had asked, pointing straight down Fifty-first Street and into the sun going down across the river.

"See what?" Frannie answered.

"You tell me what you see."

Frannie was exhausted from the day's work, her eyes weary from the computer screen, from lining up columns of figures. She blinked, looked across the river again and finally said, "I see the sun burning out in the industrial haze of New Jersey."

Genevieve laughed and gently took her arm. "You could see it that way," she said, "but look again. It's a natural Rothko."

Genevieve was right. The formless sunset was spreading and fading softly into a vanishing New Jersey horizon, the light blues and pinks melded into dark purples and oranges, just like in one of the pictures on her calendar. Just like in one of the paintings she had seen at lunch.

And how should she see this now, smack-dab in the middle of the eighties; she, a secretary, meeting Maurice, her married boss at the La Guardia Holiday Inn. She wants to see it the way Viv sees it—Viv, who had bitten her lower lip and sucked in a quick breath, as her blue eyes widened. "Oh," Viv had said. Then she had offered to lend Frannie a hat from the shop, a chocolate-colored velvet beret with one long thin feather that curved around it.

Last weekend Maurice had given her a ride home from a company party at the managing director's estate in Westport. During the drive home he had talked excitedly about his favorite aperitifs, his country home in the Périgord. Then he had talked about a book—a book, he had said, about two people who were married, but not to each other, and somehow this made the relationship perfect.

"You know," he had said, "I want to know and love many people in my life."

Frannie had been surprised that men still talked like this. But when he waited for her response, she knew she was supposed to offer her own reason for the arrangement, but all she could think to say was, "Sounds good to me," so she didn't say anything. She let him kiss her good-night.

Monday he left her a note telling her that he'd be away on business, and would she like to meet him for a drink when his flight got in on Friday? He would have a couple of hours before he had to be home. That was the day Paula, an officious junior executive, had made Frannie retype a memo six times; each time Paula had calculated the numbers wrong. Frannie had tucked Maurice's note in the breast pocket of her jacket; she touched it once in a while to make sure it was still there.

Tuesday she threw his note away. Surely it was the only thing to do.

Wednesday, after she had had dinner with Viv in SoHo, she got stuck in the subway under the East River. The lights in the train went out, and for forty-five minutes she sat there with Viv's hatbox in her lap, adjusting her eyes to the dark, trying to plan the quickest route to La Guardia on the half-torn subway map in front of her, which was obscured by the darkness and spray-painted graffiti.

Thursday she took a cab home but got stuck in a traffic jam on the Manhattan Bridge. She sat in stalled traffic, looking back at the madly sparkling city lit up like an ocean liner, and she thought of the *Tcha!* stockings that Genevieve had given her, now tucked away in her linen drawer with a rose-scented sachet. She planned her outfit to go with the stockings, an amethyst-colored, short-waisted jacket and a creamy silk blouse the same color as the stockings; all would go well with Viv's borrowed hat.

Frannie orders another drink, a Manhattan, straight up, which tastes fine, though it comes in a martini glass.

"Salut, ma petite," Maurice says when he sees her, and she wonders why she doesn't mind being called his little one. He tells her he likes her hat.

"What are you drinking?" he asks.

"A Manhattan," she answers, laughing, having never before now really thought about it.

"I'm glad," he says. "I hate all these people who drink Perrier with lime."

I do too, she thinks, but not for the same reasons you do.

He says he is happy to see her, that he had worried that she might not come, but then, they understood each other, didn't they? Underneath the table he runs his hands along her buttery stockings. He begins to tell her some things. He's telling her how he'd like to spend as much time with her as their complicated lives will allow; as he kisses her ear, he tells her those other things, too, like how he gets so aroused around her. What Frannie likes is that she really doesn't have to say anything at all. As he says those things in her ear, she can shut her eyes to the mauve upholstery and the mirrors and the ferns and the businesspeople at the bar, and she can breathe in and squeeze his hand. She can smell the opulent, otherworldly scent of bourbon and tobacco from his cigarette left burning in the ashtray, and she doesn't have to say anything at all to what he is telling her.

Maurice finally asks, "Shall we go upstairs?" And with the earnest desire of any secretary half in love with her boss, she can only think to say, "Sounds good to me."

The only way out through the bar is past the pilot and the flight attendant, and Frannie sees that the flight attendant is not a flight attendant; instead of a thin wool blazer, she has a more substantial jacket, with four bands on her sleeve and golden captain's wings on her lapel.

She had assumed that Maurice would have arranged the room beforehand, that he would have the key, so that she wouldn't have to stand beside him at the registration desk as she's doing now, while he pays for the room in cash ($175). The clerk runs down the list of questions she's reading from the computer screen, asking them if they'd like a wake-up call, help with their luggage, one bed or two.

The woman behind the counter is smart, perky, and unsuspicious; she hardly glances at Frannie. Her hair is cut short; she's wearing a blouse with a large bow in front and a sailor's collar, and when she hands Maurice the key, it's not like she's thinking, "This happens all the time," but rather, she's not thinking anything at all about these two people before her, the man with a wedding band, the girl without, the difference in their ages, Maurice's little overnight case, Frannie's lack of luggage. The glare of the computer screen reflects off the clerk's glasses so that Frannie cannot see her eyes as the woman concentrates on the screen, pushes a button, waits for something to print. With one efficient, unblinking move, she snaps the receipt out of the printer, offers one copy to Maurice, and lightly places the other in a leather in-tray.

"Enjoy your stay," she says with a bright smile.

When they get to their floor, Frannie wonders if it's too late to tell Maurice that she's lost her nerve. She hesitates; he takes her arm, gently guiding her down the hallway.

"Maurice," she says, but what can she say now? She would like to say, "Isn't it too bad that all the nice old hotel bars across the country have closed?" Then she thinks that really, Maurice is lucky that they have. Yes, Maurice is lucky that the train station in Grand Island has been converted into an office building with a bar in the basement renovated to look like a bar in an old train station. Lucky for you, she thinks, as he takes the key out of his coat pocket, that the bar at the Hotel Berlingmar is now just a place where frat boys slum it, or I might have stayed in Grand Island.

As Maurice unlocks the door, how can she tell him that suddenly she doesn't really want to go inside—not because of his wife or because she's his secretary or because of anything about him at all, but simply because of this: she knows what the room will look like before he even opens the door.

JUNE'S RICE

To this day, Aunt June will not eat rice. At restaurants, when a waitress says that a dish is served "over rice," we have all seen June look down into her menu, slightly shake her head, and murmur, "Nope—not for me." It has been more than forty years since rice has passed her lips.

When June was three, her father abandoned the family. Her mother did what she could with the small farm, but it was the thirties; the only food consistently on the table was rice. Rice as cereal for breakfast, soup with rice for dinner, rice, rice, rice, maybe some ham on Sunday, but always, always the rice.

"Oh, we had plenty of chickens," June would say, "but eggs, you see, were seventy-five cents a dozen. Who could afford to eat a chicken when you could get six-odd cents an egg? All the good stuff went to the mortgage."

When she was twenty, June married my uncle Ervin, who was by no means rich.

Still, he had meat on his table every day.

In a box in the attic I found June's yellowed wedding veil, with a few hollow grains of rice in the moth-eaten lace. As the congregation threw rice on their wedding day, Aunt June must have just smiled. "That's right," she must have thought, "you throw that rice into the air and onto the ground, in the street—until it's all gone. Feed it to the birds, for all I care. You won't be seeing it on my table again."

ALL THE BEST

On Christmas Eve day, Mom and I spend half the afternoon setting the table, with some great-aunt's embroidered tablecloth, various patterns of china and crystal, and a mishmash of all the family's heirloom silver, some engraved with initials we do not recognize. I have always been proud that out of all the fading old-money families I know who live on this side of Kansas City, ours is the only one that does not have eighteen matching place settings of sterling. Even in our better days, I wonder if we ever did.

My parents' dining room has walls a little lighter than robin's egg blue; the curtains and valences are cream-colored with threads of sienna embroidery running through them. Our entire house has always been decorated in an unlikely manner that they somehow manage to pull off; it's a house that is exquisite but touchable. I've tried to hold on to these effects in all my wallpaper designs: exquisite, touchable, risky.

We take our time choosing who's going to sit where, who will enjoy which silverware. We give my cousin Dirk the skinny "Tiki" set, the silver with the primitive design that looks like it belongs on a bamboo bowl. We laugh about how fifteen or so years ago Dirk might have sat there, mesmerized by the design, tapping into some sort of drug-induced, primordial connection. We know that tonight he won't even notice.

"I'd love to know who in our family bought this set," my mom says, squinting into the angry faces.

"Probably somebody whose weird genes I inherited," I say, making a face to imitate the design.

Mom stops and looks at me from across the table. She's very touchy on this subject, me. "Phillip, what's that supposed to mean?" she asks.

"It's a joke, Mom," I say.

"The Tiki gene," she says. "We've all got it, I suppose." She laughs, framing her eyes with deep wrinkles, lines that are news to me.

When Mom turned fifty last year she cut her straight, long, strawberry blond hair into a chin-length bob. "More my age," she said. "But put me out of my misery if I ever get one of those dandelion-puff dos." She lowered her voice to a whisper and added, "Like Alice." Alice is Mom's youngest sister, but as Mom always said, Alice was *born* old.

For Dirk's wife, Mom chooses the frilliest, most ornate, scalloped-edged, scrawly-engraved silver we have. "Jennifer will be dressed in some flowery, Edwardian-wallpaper Laura Ashley-type fabric, no doubt," Mom says. Jennifer is Dirk's wife, and for her I think the scrawly set is a good match, too— Jennifer, with her long curly golden hair that goes all over the place, the way she paints her lips a sweet pink. For our own family we choose the Deco silver, with these thin, top-of-a-clamshell lines. Julia and Frank and Alice and Mike get the Damask Rose, with the fourteen-karat detail.

It's not as if we expect anyone to notice who gets what. Usually we don't even bother matching up individual place settings, but this year is different. I'm making dinner; tonight it's my show. I've decided to pull out all the stops.

Last summer when I came out to my family, the reactions varied. My cousin Dirk actually dropped his jaw, and asked me when "it" happened. My little sister, Cookie, shrugged and said, "Well, I guess that makes sense." My mother squeezed my hand and said she was glad I thought I could tell them these things. My father said, "Phil, you're still my son, no matter what."

Back in Portland this year, I got the usual Christmas cards from each family, saying as always that they were looking forward to getting together. So home I've come, wondering how it will be different now that they've settled into their new ideas of me. I'm prepared to be sort of a red herring, I guess, but in an already fishy family.

This year I've changed the menu: Rock Cornish game hens stuffed with apricots and wild rice, and pureed leeks and potatoes. Aunt Julia is bringing her green salad with sherry vinaigrette dressing, Aunt Alice a flourless chocolate cake. It should all go together pretty well; besides, we were never truly a turkey-and-dressing kind of family.

They come back to me like snapshot pictures, past Christmases. Dad on all fours, trying to get the dog to put a cigar in his mouth. There's me balancing a full turkey platter on my head. There's Cookie, with a wide, half-toothless laugh, with Uncle Mike tickling her. There's Dirk, pretending to pick his nose, pulling out a currant. The house was always a blur of giggling women being chased by drunken uncles with meatforks, kids jumping on furniture, dogs barking at children, children barking at dogs.

We are a little late getting everything ready; worse yet, everyone arrives on time. Our family, on time. Really, just a few minutes after seven and they're all there, Cookie taking coats, Dad pouring drinks, my aunts in the kitchen gushing over the game hens just then being put into the oven.

"Aren't we eating at seven-thirty?" Alice asks.

"No, more like eight," Mom answers.

"More like eight-thirty," I say.

"You should have told me," Alice says. "I'd have brought some hors d'oeuvres. The children will be starving."

My mother pulls me aside and tells me to go put some nuts out for the kids. "I didn't even think of hors d'oeuvres," she says.

"Why would you?" I ask. "We never offer hors d'oeuvres. Snacks will be fine. Nuts—whatever, Mom."

Mom keeps asking if I'll turn the oven up and cook the hens a little faster. I'm pissed at Aunt Alice for getting Mom worried like that. Alice has always played the role of Gestapo officer in our family, but only in the past few years has anyone paid any attention to her.

When we were younger, Alice was the only aunt who ever yelled at us kids, the one who would get really mad when we drew on the walls or tore her pillowcases by jumping around in them.

We used to give Aunt Alice a hard time about how uptight she was. One summer, the kids sat around figuring out when it was each of our parents got married and then exactly when their first kid was born. Everyone checked in pretty legitimate, in those terms, except for Alice and Mike, who had Aaron six and a half months after they were married. It really bothered Alice that we figured it out, so finally she let it be known (in sterile, polite terms that I don't recall) that she too had been a virgin when she married. That is, he didn't actually penetrate her; they were just heavily messing around and he, well, came a bit too close, so to speak.

This of course made things worse, all of us running around calling Aaron "Jesus," he being immaculately conceived.

Alice was also the one who convinced Aunt Julia, years ago, that she should put Dirk into drug rehab.

"It's just marijuana," Julia said. "If they put every kid who smoked pot in drug rehab, there'd be nobody left in school!"

"But it leads to harder drugs," Alice said.

"Oh, for God's sake!" Julia said. "It's harmless stuff—if I were seventeen, I'd probably try it."

"I'm sure you would," Alice said.

They had called me in on the conversation because I was the good kid, the one in the swing choir and chess club, the two most unhip groups one could be in back then.

"Phillip," Julia asked, "what do you think?"

There was no denying he smoked pot. Everyone knew that. "I think Dirk gets better grades stoned than ninety-eight percent of the kids get straight," I said.

"See?" Aunt Julia said to Alice.

"But he could be better than everyone if he didn't smoke at all," Alice said.

Alice finally won out six months later, but only after Julia found a sock full of white cross in his underwear drawer. Though now most people would say Alice was right, it was different back then. Even the psychiatrists were reluctant to put Dirk through rehab, since he really wasn't addicted to anything but the times.

At eight-thirty we finally sit down. We are a little cranky and impatient, I guess, but the meal itself is perfect; the golden-brown hens glow from the candlelight of our tarnished candelabras.

Here's what I came back for: a dozen or so of us sitting around the long table, pulled out as far as it will go, then extended even farther with a card table. I like the way in our family that no one in particular has been relegated to the card table, not the children, not the now-adult cousins. I like the way ten conversations go all at once, how you can be in about three at the same time, how you can ease in and out of a bunch of dirty jokes, skewed political arguments fired by made-up facts, family lore, and drunken opinions on anything from the silverware to the president.

But this Christmas Eve, here we are, taking turns around the table, one of us at a time telling everyone about ourselves, about this year's new promotions, new purchases: Alice and Mike tout the benefits of their cold-water coffee press; Dirk talks about how jewel-green is the "in" color for minivans. Another cousin talks about how he's going to track mountain lions in California for his next summer vacation (I want to say that this sounds more like a job than a vacation, but I don't think my family's in the mood). Others talk about the hardships endured in purchasing this year's hot new toy. When I point out that the shortage was probably just a ploy by toy manufacturers to make people run to the store and stock up, someone says, "Phillip, don't wreck our Christmas with your Portland cynicism."

What Portland has to do with cynicism, I'm not sure, but thankfully, Cookie comes to my rescue with one of our family's still-good-for-a-laugh stories. This one is about how Mom, in her girlhood, accidentally burned down the neighbor's garage full of forties' memorabilia and collectibles. Everyone laughs, and as usual, someone laments what those "ancient" collectibles would be worth today.

"It wasn't *that* long ago," says Mom. It's the punch line she always ends the story with, but this year, she adds quietly, "Well, come to think of it, it was."

Never one to give up on a good time, Cookie brings up the Hannah story.

Once we kids watched this TV show about a catatonic child named Hannah. Someone said that Cookie looked exactly like Hannah, so we started calling Cookie Hannah; of course, she screamed and cried and ran into her room and shut the door and wouldn't come out.

When Mom asked what was the matter with Cookie, we said, "We don't know. She's really sad today. It seems the only thing that will cheer her up is if you call her Hannah." So Mom knocks on the door and says, "Hannah, dear? It's Mommy.

What's the matter?" Cookie bawls her head off while Mom's trying to comfort her, saying, "Now, now, Hannah. There, there, Hannah sweetie."

It must be the hundredth time Cookie's told this story, but it's a good one and it has the family rolling, as always. Finally, we became what we once were, a family who will stoop to anything for a laugh. I'm tempted to launch into the story of how Dirk had a hit of acid smuggled into him while he was in drug rehab; we've been known to have a collective snicker or two about this before. But perhaps this is not the time.

Instead, I tell a story that has been bouncing around in my head for years. I ask Dirk if he remembers the "hunting trip of the mind." I think he's afraid that this has something to do with his small-time druggie past, though it doesn't.

"No, Phil," he says. "I think that was in *your* mind."

"No," I say. "When I was eight and you were ten, one summer in the Ozarks you kept telling me that your dad was going to come down and take you hunting—"

"You can't hunt there in the summer," Uncle Frank says, interrupting.

"Well, I didn't know that *then,*" I say. "Anyway, Dirk kept telling me how Uncle Frank was going to come down and take him hunting and did I want to come along? Dirk, you described it so vividly. I can still see the rifles with their shiny wood, the way you said we'd tie the deer to the top of the car. I mean, you'd spend rainy afternoons telling me how we'd have to go deep into the woods, how we'd have to hike for a few days to get to this really good place where all the wild turkeys and red foxes and pheasants thrived. We'd have to catch all our food, the three of us. You'd said you'd put me in charge of catching the fish we'd eat for breakfast . . ."

I get a bit carried away, I'm sure, with my memory of this description that was just in the head of a young boy playing a trick on his younger cousin. But I tell the family the whole elaborate tale, as Dirk told me and as I have carried it around with me all these years, even after I knew it was only a joke. The green-green grass, the wormy smell of the stream we'd fish from, the stream we'd bathe in. How we'd wash our clothes every two days because we could only take one change of clothes with us.

"Phillip," Dirk interjects, "are you sure this trip, or my telling it, wasn't just in your head?"

"That's the point," I tell him. "That summer I kept asking you each day, 'Is this the day we go hunting?' And each day you'd say, 'No, not today. Maybe tomorrow.' Finally, I asked Mom and Aunt Julia when Uncle Frank would come down and take us hunting, and of course they didn't know anything about it. They asked you and you said, 'I don't know, he's been talking about some hunting trip for *weeks*! I don't know where he got the idea.' "

This should have my family in stitches. I mean, we kids did this kind of stuff all the time to each other. But they're just sitting there, politely listening, while I'm trying to think of a punch line.

"That's *cold,* man," one of the kids at the table finally says.

After a while, Aunt Alice adds, "I guess that's one nice thing about getting old. You start to forget all those awful little things that happened to you when you were young." She begins to get up, flinging her napkin aside, and says, "Well, these dishes aren't going to wash themselves." Others begin to ease back from the table.

"But it wasn't awful," I say. "It's funny and it's strange, but it's not awful, that story. The way Dirk told me about the woods, it was like I'd been there. Dirk, you're a born story-teller. Even after I found out it was a trick, I would still think about it and get all ready to go, in my mind. Hell, I was glad just to be in the story! I still think about that trip sometimes, even now."

But no one responds, and suddenly the clearing of the dishes becomes an urgent, pressing need; I sit watching the frenzy until I am offered solace by five-year-old Daphne tugging at my hand and wanting me to go look at her new Barbie.

Aunt Julia inherited all the family portraits. There was one I begged her for, one I finally got. It is of the Morgan brothers, my great-grandfather and his brother, who started the Morgan Brothers Office Supply business in the 1920s, a business that thrived until my grandfather sold out in the early 1980s.

The portrait shows two serious, straight-off-the-boat young men with a direct, ready-to-work earnestness about them. It's not just because of who they were that I wanted the pictures. It's not just their stern, horizontal-lined smileless mouths that intrigue me, nor their identical cowlicks we've all inherited. It's not even the smoothness of the brown-tone print set in a carved cardboard mat, or how their direct, furrowed-brow stares will always look out but tell us nothing.

No, what I love is how these two must have decided one day to go down to Woltz's Studios and get their portraits taken together. No wives, no kids, just those two in their Sunday best, billowy white shirts with English collars, tie clips, and vests. We don't know that much about them, but we do know that for some reason they wanted to have their picture taken together. Not just a yearly snapshot around a Christmas tree, but something they'd want us to look at generations later.

I have but one picture of just Dirk and me, taken in a photo booth at Riverbend Park when we were about twelve and fourteen. To those who might look on it years from now, we will be just two sweaty boys in T-shirts with shiny summer tans. It was taken the last summer before Dirk started hanging around with guys who spent summers driving around in Jeeps, looking for girls.

A few years later, when they finally did put Dirk into rehab, I went to visit him. It was a shorter inpatient treatment for nonaddicted heavy users. I remember thinking if I looked at him one way, I could see him lying there, sallow and strung out underneath white sheets, in trouble. But if I looked at him another way, he was just the Dirk that I'd always known, momentarily bleached out by an ugly gown, bad food, a hideously beige room, and a lot of people trying to convince him he had serious problems.

"Listen," he said then, "I want you to do me a favor. You know my girlfriend, Janet. She's going to give you a letter for me. You take it, give it to my mom, and tell her it's from you. That way she can bring it in and they won't search it."

I was sure he was up to something, but I also had enough faith in him to know that he was fine, just Dirk, misplaced for a while. I knew he'd never waste away as a drug addict; I also knew I'd do anything for him.

For years and until it recently became impossible to talk about these things, we'd have a laugh about the hit of blotter acid Aunt Julia unwittingly smuggled in to Dirk while he was in drug rehab.

When I moved to Portland, the rest of the family had about as much faith in me as they did in Dirk during his drug days. They'd say things like, "If you're still waiting tables in a year, you can always move back."

But not Dirk. The night before I left, he came to visit me. I've never told anyone this, but I was terrified of leaving town and terribly sad to be leaving my family. Dirk doesn't know this, but he talked me into leaving just by saying to me, "Phil, I wish you all the best in the world, and I have no doubt you'll find it." He seemed almost envious, briefly, even though he was well into his insurance career and I was off to wait tables in Portland.

Sometimes now when I think of Dirk I can't imagine how we ended up so different—different from each other and different from the two tanned boys at Riverbend Park. I'm glad that Dirk doesn't do drugs anymore; his drug rehab acid story is only funny because he's now so far out of danger. Still, I'd like to know when everyone got so afraid—and I can't help but think that I somehow fuel their fears.

And then I think of how Dirk said that—"I wish you all the best"—back when I needed it most, and how easily that assuaged my fears. I wish I could do the same for him.

Mom, Aunt Alice, and I do the dishes, scraping off the plates, throwing the still- meaty bones and half-full bird cavities into a big, greasy plastic bag. Aunt Alice says something about how it's silly to go to all the trouble of cooking such a feast. Next year, she says, at her house we'll eat off paper plates so we can spend more time enjoying each other rather than doing dishes.

Everyone had said a perfunctory, "Mmmm, this is good, Phillip." But from the silverware left on the plates when they were brought into the kitchen, I can pretty much tell who ate what. The children were most systematic, picking aside the apricots, but that's just kids, carving out their tastes. The adults ate here and there, gave each dish a hearty try, but almost no one ate more than half of what I served.

"The thing about Cornish game hens," Mom says, "is that the guests can't choose what size portions they want."

I can't remember ever thinking of my aunts, uncles, and cousins as guests. I'd like to think that Mom was right, that it was just too much food. Wild rice does have a way of expanding in your stomach.

"I thought it was great, Phillip," Mom says. She has never been a huge eater, so I don't mind that she only picked at a few bits. She used to have a cigarette going through most every meal, but lately, and tonight, she just sat there, swirling the Vouvray in her glass, lightly forking the rice now and then, wishing, I'm sure, that it was still acceptable to smoke at the dinner table.

"I just want you to know," Aunt Julia says as we're packing away the silverware, "I have always admired alternative lifestyle sorts of people." Aunt Julia has always been the hip (or at least, trendy) one, even back when we were teenagers. She was the one who smoked long, brown cigarettes and brought Brie and wine to family picnics. She is the only one in our family reputed to have had an affair. Long after it was over, I'd hear her mentioning it to my mom. "Believe me," she said, rolling her eyes, "adultery isn't all it's cracked up to be."

"Your grandfather," Julia says now, "he wouldn't be having any of this, the old fart."

"I don't know about that," I say.

"Don't fool yourself," she says. "He still used the 'n word' for blacks. Phillip, he'd be rolling in his grave."

I try to tell her how Granddad was a bit off his nut all his life. He wasn't that white-haired venerable citizen he looked. "Remember how he used to cheat us kids at cards? Really cheat, as much as he could get by with, even when we were really little. He loved to cheat. He'd play to cheat, and he'd *actually* take our pennies. He wouldn't say, 'No, that's okay, you keep your money,' like most grandfathers. He'd gather up our pennies, laughing."

"Still," Aunt Julia says, "you've got to admit that Granddad would never have gone for this alternative sexuality stuff."

It's useless to enlist support from a dead man, but I still think he'd be with me on this. In spite of how I didn't fit the program—my refusal to go to church, dropping out of college for a while to join a mime troupe, going back to major in art—it was *me* whom he willed his gold watch to. Out of a son, three daughters, and ten grandchildren, I've got it, that pocket watch with its ornate swirl design, now almost gone, worn away from all those years of rubbing on the inside of his pockets.

Our conversation shifted to now.

"Just what is it you're doing these days, Phillip?" she asks.

In Portland, I am an interior designer, or more specifically, I paint wallpaper. This is what I do, eight to ten hours a day: design wallpaper. It has taken me five years to build a portfolio of twelve designs that I can finally say are joyful, perfect, exactly what I want to share.

So far, only one of my designs is on anyone's walls. I also work, four hours a day, as an orderly at a Portland hospital in the cardiac recovery ward. Though the wallpapers I have designed say more about me than anything, Aunt Julia wants to hear about my job.

"Are you still a nurse?" she asks.

"I'm not even a nurse," I say. "I'm an orderly."

"Any chance for promotion?"

"Yes, well, I got passed over for a cardiologist position this year, but I'm hoping for better luck next year."

I try to tell Julia about my wallpaper, the one that someone actually has in his house. It won a prize, an award in a charity house show, but it was a prize that has kept me going, a prize that should have told them, "Yes, he's for real and not some limp-wristed wanna-be decorator." They need that sort of stuff, my family, and I need it, too.

So I tell Aunt Julia not just about my little prize, but about the wallpaper, how I based the design on the swirls on grandfather's watch. I take out a piece of paper and a pen and I ask, "Remember the pinwheels that were engraved on it?"

"No, not really."

"Well, they were like this," I say, drawing the swirling spirals for her. "I painted them in ocher and brown, which went with the furnishings in the room: olive, wheat, gold, celedon, and mahogany. Because when I walked into that room, it looked very pressed and calm, so I thought of Granddad and I designed the wallpaper to balance the stateliness of the room with the whimsy that could also be him—like the whimsy in his watch, with its frills."

She asks me if I have mass-marketed the wallpaper.

"No," I explain. "Not yet. It was a charity piece. An AIDS benefit." I explain how a bunch of designers got together and redid this rich guy's house for his $250,000 contribution. "I got to do the wallpaper, and it has garnered some commissions, but no one has bought the rights to the paper yet."

"AIDS—such a good cause," she says. She gives me that concerned look that all relatives and old friends give me when I tell them I'm gay.

"Yes, Julia," I say. "I know you're wondering. I'm negative."

"What a relief, Phillip. We all worry about you."

"Don't worry about me," I say, and getting back to the wallpaper, I ask her, "Would you like me to send you a slide of the room? I'd like to know it reminds you as much of Granddad as it did me."

"Phil," she says, not listening, "do you still have Granddad's watch?"

"What do *you* think?"

"I'm just asking."

"Well, Julia," I say, giving her the most serious, shameful look I can muster, "I wish you hadn't asked. I am not proud to tell you that, you know, things have been a little rough for me this year, me being just an orderly and all—"

"And?"

"Well," I continue, "I had to pawn it to buy some groceries last month."

"Phillip, how could you? It's a family heirloom. Any one of us would have bought it from you and kept it in the family."

"Sorry," I say. "I was hungry."

"So how much did you get for it?"

"Fifty bucks," I tell her. "Not much, I know, but Portland's crawling with dead grandfathers' favorite grandsons pawning gold watches."

"You let it go for fifty bucks?" She puts her hand to her mouth, her lips trembling. She looks like she's going to cry and in her place I probably would if I really thought one of us would actually sell Granddad's watch.

"Julia," I say, pulling the watch out of my pocket. "Julia, it's me, Phil."

She looks at it, leans against me, laughing into my neck. "What am I thinking?" she says. "You'll be just fine, Phillip."

"Julia, I *am* fine."

My dad is drunk, on what he calls his once-or-twice-a-year, big-big drunk. Everyone else has gone home or to bed, and we are in the den, which is dark except for the lights of the Christmas tree. We talk a little about Portland, my prospects in design. I tell him about the new apartment Rich and I have moved into.

"Phillip," he says slowly, "I *love* women." He sighs, as if to say, there, I've said it; as if that were *his* big secret.

"I know, Dad."

"No, I really mean it. I love women. I'd never cheat on your mother, that's not the point. But I want you to know it. I love women." He clinks his ice around in his glass, sucks some bourbon off a cube. "And you know something else? Women love me. They really do."

I'm not sure what to add to that.

"I just don't see it," Dad says.

"See what?"

"See how you can love men like I love women."

"It's different, Dad."

"I'll say it is!"

I do not know how to respond. I want to say, "Yes, that's right. It *is* different. I don't love men like you love women. I do

99

not love Rich like you love Mother. And Aunt Julia's love for Uncle Frank is different from yours for Mom and Aunt Alice's love for Uncle Mike is all different, too."

But I know my love seems even more different because we are men. I do not know how to tell him how it is different because I have not loved a woman, so how could I explain it, the difference?

"Dad," I say instead, "I'm not sure that you're really talking about love."

This sobers him; this rocks his latent Catholic soul. He's out of his dreamy mood and I'm sorry I said it.

Christmas days at our house are pretty casual. Breakfast is glazed donuts and coffee. We open a few presents. Lunch is leftovers from the night before, but since I foolishly changed the menu last night, there are no leftovers.

Mom cooks up a favorite of Cookie's and mine, a tuna casserole with tomato slices and Parmesan cheese on top. And for two hours on Christmas Day, we sit in our little breakfast nook, the afternoon sun bright and warm and glaring in, Mom smoking cigarette after cigarette, Dad bleary-eyed and saying, as usual, that he's finished drinking forever. Though it is hardly one of those times you'd shoot a picture of to send with Christmas cards next year, I do not want this time to end.

We throw grapes into each other's mouth, green grapes left uneaten from the night before, since Julia had informed everyone that green grapes were, for some reason, politically incorrect to consume. We eat them, Mom, Dad, Cookie, and I, or at least we throw a lot of them around.

Dad opens wide, and all three of us make a clean, rimless shot into his mouth. Dad tries to chew and swallow but, with a guffaw, spits two of them across the room. Our laugh turns into a shrill, high-pitched giggle that Dad and I share; the dog is frantic, running around, barking, chasing the grapes.

Cookie's laughing so hard that milk comes out her nose, a

neat trick of hers. And then when Dad's giggle turns into a gasp, no one is all too worried. "Look, the international choking symbol," Cookie says, still laughing, as Dad beats his chest with his open palm and raises his other arm into the air, crossing his eyes and turning close to purple.

Even as I perform the Heimlich maneuver and Dad spits out a half-chewed grape, we're all laughing; we can't stop even as we wait for Dad to catch his breath.

Which he does, gasping, laughing, and breathing deeply, just as we all somehow knew he would.

On Christmas days at four, we always go over to Aunt Julia and Uncle Frank's house to spend the evening with them. This year is no different from the others: Julia makes a huge pot of chili, the kids compare toys, and we all play games that have changed with the years' fads: Uno, Trivial Pursuit, Scruples, Pictionary.

I suggest that we all watch the Super 8 movies of when we were kids, but no one has an operating Super 8 projector anymore. I make a note to have the films converted to videocassette.

After dinner, Dirk pulls me aside, squinting and looking straight into my eyes. "Phillip, I want to ask you a serious question."

"Sure," I say, looking forward to it, really. "Anything."

"Phil, we were wondering. This morning, well, we were sitting around the tree and Alice dropped by and she was all worried."

"So?"

"Well, we started talking about how you were kind of acting strangely last night, with that hunting-trip-of-the-head stuff. Alice, well, she asked me if I thought you might have been doing some drugs."

"Very fucking funny," I say. I really thought he was kidding.

"Phil, just answer me."

And so I answer. "Why didn't you tell her, Dirk? Why didn't you tell her what kind of drugs I was on last night, because you'd know, wouldn't you, considering you got high every Christmas from the age of fourteen to twenty-five. You used to accuse me of being some sort of wimp because I wouldn't get high with you."

He grabs my shoulder and tells me to quiet down. "Phillip, it's okay. I don't care if you were on drugs, but it would explain a lot."

"Explain what? Like why I wasn't acting like you?"

"Shhh, Phil. It's all right."

"Let me picture this," I say. "Christmas morning, right? You're all—"

"Not *us*, Phil. You. Were you on drugs? Are you now?"

"Your whole family is sitting around the tree this morning. Opening presents, the sun's shining in. Dirk, hasn't this been one of the sunniest, most beautiful Christmases ever?"

"Yeah, it's been a nice one, Phillip."

"But you miss all that, don't you?"

"Settle down, Phillip," Dirk keeps saying.

"Because Alice comes over. Maybe she's just walking over to wish you a Merry Christmas or to borrow a cup of sugar or something nice like that. But instead she's worried and for some reason you all care for once."

"She's concerned. That's all."

"Am I getting this right? So Alice consults you, the resident drug expert. She says, 'I'm worried about Phil. He acted so strangely last night. Could it be that he might have been on drugs? *He wasn't acting like us, so maybe he was on drugs.*'"

"Just forget it, all right?" He tries to walk away, but I grab his arm.

"And what did you say, Dirk?"

"I told them I'd talk to you."

"Don't talk to me, Dirk. Talk to Alice and Mike and Julia

102

and Frank and your sister and her husband and the kids and tell them, '*No, Phil is not on drugs.*' Go tell them that it's Phil, just being Phil, one of us, our flesh and blood."

"Why do you think we worry? That's why we're concerned—"

"Yes, that's why you worry. I'm your flesh and blood, and that makes you worried, that's what bothers you most."

I'm acting like a lunatic, I know. But it's not like no one has ever blown up at Christmas in our family. Every few years a sister gets mad at a sister, a spouse yells at a spouse, and the kids scream all over the place. But the rage always blows over, and always, life lumps along.

But after my blowup with Dirk, the evening's over. No one takes sides. On the way home, Cookie and Mom and Dad do not tell me what an ass Dirk has become, so I don't get the chance to say, "Oh, he's fine, maybe a little uptight, but still our Dirk."

The next day as I'm packing to leave, I think of when I'll come home again. When I think of Christmases to come, I no longer know what to visualize. I can only say that I thought we'd pull it off, our family of all families. I really thought we could pull through, this large nutty family with drinkers, smokers, one-time adulterers, ex-druggies, small-time cheats, and two-bit liars, this once-prominent family with no matching silver, all of us all over the place, but not one of us outside.

On the flight home I try to think of ways to keep my family from worrying about me.

Maybe I should try to blend. Buying a lot of great stuff so I have something nonthreatening to talk about around the dinner table would help, but that's not in this year's fiscal plan, I'm afraid.

Another tactic: come back and act like the flamboyant queen that I am not, cramming my difference down their throats.

But I won't do that, either. All I can do is to come home and endure and hope for the best: those few sunny hours in the breakfast nook, wrought with stale breath, hangovers, secondhand smoke, and maybe even a few moments of risk where we can all once again prove our faith. After all that's happened, I'm even starting to look forward to next Christmas.

FRED'S BEER

Grandmother had no time for men who drank, and no one in the family ever found out why. She often said that she waited until she was twenty-eight to get married because it took her that long to find a man who didn't drink. "I'd sooner have been an old maid," she would often say, "than to have married a drinker."

It was after some argument, then, that she finally agreed to let her son keep a few bottles of beer cooling in the icebox for his all-night forays into town. "Ma," he had said, "in three weeks, I'll be flying over who-knows-where. What do a few beers in your icebox matter now?" It was August 1943; Fred was a U.S. Air Force captain, home on leave. Even so, she wouldn't let him drink his beers inside the house.

When his buddies picked him up that day to drive him back to the base, Grandma told him he forgot something. "Fred, look here," she said. "I don't want this is my house." She tried to hand him that one remaining bottle of beer.

"No, not now. Mama, you keep it cold for me and I'll drink it when I come home."

"Like fun I'll keep it in my house," she said. But as Fred

105

walked toward the car, she called out her promise after him. "Okay, then," she said. "I'll keep it for you. It'll be here, nice and cold."

In March 1944, Fred was reported missing, shot down over North Africa. Then he was reported to be dead, buried outside Rome. A few years later, my grandparents had his remains exhumed and finally laid to rest in his hometown, but as Grandma would say, "Who knows whose bones are in that coffin?" I don't think she was ever entirely convinced they were Fred's.

Over the years Fred's beer was moved around the house, from the icebox to a refrigerator, to the cool storage cellar, and finally to the back of a dark cupboard in the pantry behind some cleaning supplies. If someone found it and brought it out and asked Grandma what it was there for, she'd tell them about Fred's beer. And then she'd say, "Now put it back."

She died on what would have been Fred's seventy-second birthday; she herself was one hundred and one.

During the week we cleaned out her house, I came across Fred's beer. The rusting cap had become so thin and fragile I could almost dent it with a touch of my fingers. I displayed the beer on the kitchen counter, next to the utensils, glassware, and dishes we were dividing up among the relatives. I was hoping, I guess, that someone would claim it, that someone had an idea of what to do with it now.

Everyone knew just what it was. Each of us would spot it on the counter, pick it up, turn it around carefully in our hands and say, "Fred's beer."

And then we'd put it back.

When it came time to close up the house for good, no one had claimed Fred's beer. Not knowing what else to do with it, I put it in a box of utensils to take home with me.

But it didn't belong there.

I thought of Grandma on that hot summer's day, waving good-bye to Fred, going back into her house, and putting his beer in the icebox. I thought of how she saved his beer for forty years, in spite of how she felt about drinking. I thought how if your son was killed in a war, you'd want to think for as long as you could that maybe there was some mistake, that someday he might just come walking through the porch door and say, "Now, Mama, where's that beer?" And you could tease him once again. "You're not drinking that in my house."

I didn't take Fred's beer. Instead, I put it back in the dark corner of the empty cupboard. Against the quiet of the still farm I could almost hear what she'd say. "You put that back now. Fred ain't come home yet." I left it where she left it, waiting.

MARLON HENLEY

When I first told my mother I was seeing Marlon Henley again, all she cared to remember about him were the pants he wore twenty-some-odd years ago.

"He always wore those gauzy hippie pants. You remember? Those Pakistani harem thingies."

"Did you know he's writing a column for the newspaper?"

"And no underwear. You could always see what was underneath, or at least the outline of it flopping around. Didn't matter if he was standing or sitting, it was always *there*."

"He writes about recycling."

"They were like pajamas! Imagine, men dressing like that."

"Well, he doesn't dress like that anymore. He's back in town and he writes about all the ways you can recycle—"

"And those sandals he wore. Made him look like Jesus Christ."

The reasons my mother and I live together would seem to make sense. She's recently widowed, getting used to living in a condo with a couple of extra rooms. I'm recently divorced, getting used to half as many friends, too little to do, and a short-term budget deficit. It should be a good arrangement, providing some sort of mutual enrichment, and sometimes it is that way. But more and more lately I've felt urges that I've long ago forgotten, like the urge right now to put my fingers in my ears and scream, "I can't hear you! I can't hear you! I can't hear you!"

I ask her if she wants something to eat. I go to the kitchen, hoping to steer her away from the subject of this quilt she made, but from the kitchen I hear her say, "You know, that quilt is going to make an interesting artifact someday. Well, it already is!" Her voice trails off toward the linen closet and I wonder when people started collecting old things because they were quirky, oddball, and funny—if they always did, or if it's only the stuff of my generation that's a big joke.

My mother's mother made more than one hundred quilts in her lifetime, no two even remotely alike. Sometimes the patterns were a little hokey, like ladies in hoop skirts or butterflies; still, I always admired the way she'd make order out of the tawdry scraps.

My mother has made one quilt in her life and it has no pattern. It is a crazy quilt she made from scraps of all the clothes our family wore in the 1960s and 1970s, uneven pieces scattered in an uneven pattern: a long curving swirl cut from her purple polyester pants next to a big square that was once a lime-green polka dot scarf, next to some South American gauze from a shirt of mine, next to a triangle cut from a wide psychedelic tie I gave my father that he never wore. It's not as ugly as it is curious. It's more interesting to me than my high school yearbook, but Mother seems to pull it out of the linen closet mostly for a good laugh.

"Laurie, look," she says. "There's that piece, right here, of those harem pants he used to wear. Marlon Henley's harem pants."

We often have this argument. Yes, they could be those pants—I had worn his clothes, probably kept some, and yes, he had sometimes worn mine, but I don't really want to get into it right now.

"That was a blouse," I say.

"I'm sure that was those pants. I particularly remember that purple-and-orange motif working through the pattern. Weren't you kids silly?"

"It was a blouse," I say as I fold the quilt up and go on trying to tell her about Marlon now.

Which is that he's back from Oregon. Three weeks ago I saw him at the paper where I work at the copy desk. I had heard he was around, writing a column on recycling tips and environmental issues. When I heard he was back, I kept looking out for him, but the day he stood at my desk and smiled at me it took me a second to be sure it was him.

"Well, here we are, twenty years closer to death," he said. He always did make me laugh.

He still wears wire-frame glasses, not round, but oval, which are now back in style, I guess. He has long black hair, just as thick and curly as ever, but now it glistens with gray— not the dull gray of the elderly, but a shiny, metallic, flashy gray that makes his hair look even wirier and more out of control than before. To me he looked not just twenty years older, but evolved. People always tell me that I look the same as I did in high school, and I wonder if this means I look young or just hopelessly out of sync.

Mother insists our getting back together is just a fling. "You like each other because you remind one another of when you were younger," she said. "The attraction will dry up soon enough, and you'll find you won't have anything in common nowadays."

Mom's always wrong about these things—not about the outcome, but the reason things happen. Twenty years ago, Marlon and I went to Boulder together for spring break. Mom said then that he would drop me as soon as we got back. "You can't go traipsing halfway across the country with a man and expect him to respect you after *that*."

"After what?"

"You know as well as I do that you'll end up in bed together sometime during that trip."

I laughed out loud. "Mom, times have changed."

"Times have changed," she said. "Men don't change."

Marlon and I broke up soon after the trip. Mom wasn't right, he didn't drop me because of the trip, but he did leave. He left that summer because he wanted to finish school out west. I didn't want to leave town, for there is nothing wrong with this town. And if I stay here long enough, maybe everyone who left will move back. Marlon Henley did.

After two months, Mom has to admit it's more than a fling. She starts to read his column, and sometimes she even quotes him. She invites him to dinner.

"Looks like I'll have to get out my old vegetarian cookbook," she says.

"Oh, he's not vegetarian anymore."

She smiled. "No, I don't suppose he would be."

She insists on making dinner that night, a Thai stir-fry that is one of my recipes.

"I'll have to tell Marlon that I've been recycling since way before it came into fashion," she says while she masterfully cuts green, yellow, and red bell peppers into uniform strips. "I've always saved scraps of tinfoil. I rinse out Glad bags and use them again and again—"

"Do you think that's sanitary?"

"I always save twist ties and rubber bands and—"

"That'll save a lot of space in the land fill," I say.

"At work I discourage Styrofoam cups in my department. I gave all my people coffee mugs one year for Christmas. And these women today who put plastic diapers on their babies? I used cloth diapers on you kids, and when you were finished, I had dust rags for years."

I want to remind her that before she called it recycling,

she called it saving a buck, but I don't, for I'm glad she's recycling. Still, it's nothing to be proud of. I mean, it seems to me we've got into this whole recycling thing because somewhere along the line, we really messed up, not because we're such kind and gentle geniuses.

Outside on the balcony, there is a new sound. Above the din of her chatter and the steady traffic outside, I hear wind chimes in the breeze. It's not the tinny tinkling of glass chimes, but a low, lingering sound—solemn, like church carillons. I can see the chimes have five long tubes made of uneven dull gray metal. They look strong, like they'd make beautiful noise even through a tornado, like they'll last forever.

"Mom, where did you get those?"

"At the community bazaar," she says. She is smiling like she knows a secret. "Look closer at it."

The gong in the middle has some large letters indented into the metal. I look closer and I realize that the whole thing is made of old license plates, melted and shaped and spray painted an industrial gray.

"It's made of completely recycled metal!" she says, beaming, clasping her hands together like she's going to pray.

"So now you're buying someone else's junk?" I say as I dump my iced tea into the fern and head for something stronger.

"Why don't we see what your Marlon Henley thinks about it?" she asks.

Of course, Marlon thinks it's grand.

He arrives, not wearing harem pants, but tight spandex bicycle shorts and a "Just Do It" T-shirt.

We settle on the balcony with some sort of Chardonnay, and Marlon reverently gazes at the wind chimes while Mom tells him all about them.

"Next year," he says, "I'm making a vow. For one year I'm not going to buy anything made from new materials, except food. Everything I buy will be used or recycled, or I'll live without it."

"Well, that's the way we did it growing up," Mom says.

"What about toilet paper?" I ask.

"We didn't buy new things for years—"

"You can get toilet paper made from recycled paper," Marlon says.

"Growing up we saved everything. We saved every scrap of clothing, and what Mother couldn't salvage she'd make into a quilt . . ."

Oh, that damned quilt.

I creep into the kitchen. I boil the water. I add the rice, wipe down the countertops, and set the table. I spend as much time in the kitchen as I think it will take for her to start and then stop talking about the quilt, but when I go out she is saying, "And this green thing is a scarf Laurie's father gave to me . . ."

Marlon is laughing.

"Now Marlon," Mom says, "you tell me. Does this look familiar?"

It only takes him a second. "Hey," he says. "My Sri Lankan pants. I was thinking about those the other day. I loved those things."

"I just love Thai food," my mother says. Though she only says it once, it sounds like a mantra.

I must admit that she made a rather good stir-fry—at once fiery and sweet, with sparkling, crisp-tender vegetables, the chicken not a bit dry. The three of us eat with wooden chop-sticks, and I wonder where we all learned to do this, why it seems as easy to us as eating with a fork.

She didn't pay much attention to Marlon twenty years ago, but tonight she can't seem to get enough of him. She quotes things he's said in his column, asking him to elaborate. This he does, tilting back, wrapping his ankles around the legs of his chair. And of course with those spandex bicycle shorts, you can see it, the outline of it and all.

Still, Marlon is not one to talk about himself all night, so at one point he asks me if I'm going to apply for the copy chief job that has just opened up.

"I like my job," I say. "Besides, I'm not really a head-of-a-department sort of person."

"Don't you want to try something new?" he asks.

"That'll be the day," Mother says, pouring Marlon more wine.

"New," I say. "It's a newspaper. I get plenty of new. Too much new. New crimes, new floods, new celebrities, a million new ways to cook turkey. Every day there's something new, and that's plenty of new for me."

"If it were left up to people like Laurie," Mom says, "we'd all be living in grass huts."

"Well," Marlon laughs, "at least we wouldn't have to worry about recycling, would we?"

"Ha!" I say, half laughing, half surprised at an articulate defense of my unambitious self.

"I actually think you'd like that, Laurie," Mom says. "Living in a grass hut, having a guy with a grunt for a name do all the hunting and gathering for you."

"I dunno," I say. "It doesn't sound so bad. It would be especially nice being dragged around the hut by my hair."

Nothing's funny anymore. I swear Marlon would've been rolling on the floor at this twenty years ago, but now he just sits there looking at me like I've just spoken out against Greenpeace. Even Mom doesn't know what to say.

"You'd be a shoo-in for that copy chief job," Marlon finally says.

Mom starts telling Marlon how he should write a book. So I don't go into it, the fact that the copy chief job is open because they already offered it to me and I turned it down. I don't get into it, and maybe it's the wine, but instead of thinking of a promotion and listening to Marlon talk about his book, I just stare at his wiry hair, which seems to have a life of its own. Mother once accused me of being more interested in men than in my career, and tonight, she's right, because all I want right now is for her to leave and for Marlon and me to go lie down on that crazy quilt she left on the couch, go lie there together and mess it up.

When my grandfather reached his ninety-fifth birthday, we had an open house and invited everyone he knew, though there weren't that many people left. Most of the guests were at least twenty years younger than him. For two hours people he had to pretend to recognize swarmed around him, saying things like, "How's it feel to be almost a century old?" and "How did you spend New Year's Eve at the turn of the century?"

At one point I asked him, "Grandpa, if you could relive any year or any decade or any time at all, when would it be? When were you the most happy?"

He sat there in his wheelchair, expressionless for a few moments, watching the people chat and whirl around him. I wasn't sure if he had heard me. Finally, he answered, "Well, now. I'm having a good time right now. But then, it was all good."

I couldn't see it, him having such a good time now, his tiny body withered by a stroke, all the people who knew him the first decade or two of his life long gone. Still, I took his word for it.

I stand in the kitchen after Marlon leaves and I think about how it's been pretty good for me, too, most of the time. It's not like I wish we could go back to 1972 and Marlon's gauze pants, but I loved it then and then I loved being married, working with people who also liked words and news and newspapers—and that was enough for me. But then something strange happened: everyone started moving more quickly, up and away and elsewhere, and soon every conversation revolved around how busy everyone was. A year ago, my husband fell in love with his boss, and now I have a new lifestyle, a new roommate, a new boyfriend. Is it so bad to want to just stand still for a moment? For a decade?

I think of Marlon and his bicycle shorts, leaning back with his legs wrapped around his chair, and it does make me smile, until I remember that soon we'll be making fun of spandex bicycle shorts, if we aren't already.

Though she'd rather be watching Leno, Mother helps me with the dishes. She stops as I start to throw the wooden chopsticks away.

"You can save those," she says. "Just scrub them off real well."

"They're a dollar for twenty," I say, forgetting that these days the issue is ecology, not economy.

"No use wasting them," she says. "We'll use them next time Marlon comes over."

But after she leaves I throw them away because I do not want her holding them up in ten years and saying, "Remember how Thai stir-fries were the big thing? And remember how crazy you were about that Marlon Henley?"

THE SEARS AND ROEBUCK ROUND OAK TABLE

Grandmother ordered it from the catalog in May 1919; it came in on the train just in time for threshing season. It was hot that year, too hot to have all the workers in her house. She set up the heavy table outside in the front yard, shaded by the oaks, where she and the neighbor women served the men their noontime dinners.

A few years later when they paved the Lincoln Highway that went in front of her house, she fed the road crew around this table, collecting twenty-five cents from each man. "Even after the men moved on up the road to Scranton," she'd tell us, "they'd come all the way back here for their dinner."

The round oak table came with twelve leaves; it could seat four to twenty. Its everyday size changed over the years: four, five, six, to ten with her own family and the hired hands, then smaller when her children moved out, larger again when they came back, bringing children and grandchildren of their own.

It was around this table that the men would sit when they came in from the fields for their breaks.

It was around this table that they played cards at night, a variety of Pitch only this family knew.

And it was around this table that her family and neighbors stood, drinking coffee, eating cookies, reminiscing on the hot, Indian summer day after her funeral.

It was around this table, too, that her two sons and daughter discussed it, how they'd divide the estate, who'd get the old house, the buildings, the timber, and the land. They sat at this table, on the last day before the farm was split up for good, tossing out figures of acres and yields, depreciation and cash-rent values.

I wasn't supposed to be there that day, me being just one of the many grandchildren. I stayed in the attic, slowly going through boxes of postcards and buttons, letters, newspapers, photographs. What to do with all this stuff, these things someone had thought should be saved? It got so I didn't want to touch anything—I just wanted to leave everything where it belonged.

I lay down on the dusty featherbed in the attic, covering myself with a frayed quilt, one of the few someone hadn't yet claimed. From the attic I could hear raised voices below me.

"What the hell . . ."

"I'll be damned if I'm gonna . . ."

"That's not it at all . . ."

I lay there listening to Ray, the louder of the two brothers, saying, "Tillable acres. Hell, I'm talking tillable acres. You don't count the damned road!"

Their wives had not been asked to this back-and-forth of who got what; if they had, they'd still be there now, or they'd all be dead. The two weren't the best of friends, and over the past few years their mutual indifference had grown into intolerance; the brothers, who had farmed together all their lives, split up their partnership. Now Ray and Ervin hardly saw one another, though their houses faced each other across a field.

Lying on the featherbed, I drifted in and out of their arguments and then to sleep, thinking of many years back, thinking to my earliest memories of long, lingering days on the farm, breezy days of collecting wild raspberries or hickory nuts in the timber, or finding a nest of bald baby swallows in the hayloft.

When I awoke, it was quieter downstairs. I still heard the

swearwords the brothers had always used when their wives weren't around, but even Ray spoke more quietly now.

When I went downstairs, I knew they had figured it all out.

"One thing is," Ray was saying, "we're all honest, I know that."

"Like hell," Ervin said, laughing out bursts of cigarette smoke.

The sun was going down; across the field in their facing homes, their wives would be waiting for them to come home for supper, waiting to hear who got what, most likely unhappy with the results.

But for now, the two brothers sit around the oak table, smoking the cigarettes they hide from their wives. They're done talking business; it's set who's getting what. Still, they linger, arguing now over what happened which year, when it was that the first barn burned down, when they built the chicken coop, and when they stopped raising hens.

The dining room is packed full of boxes, the furniture's been labeled as to what goes where. Ray, the one they always said talked too much, keeps talking now; he's sure the timber was bought in 1920. "Horseshit," Ervin says, snuffing out his cigarette in a green depression glass ashtray. Once again, Ray says that he should get going. Still, they sit.

Ervin taps his rough fingers on the well-varnished wood of the round oak table. "So, you got this in the deal," he says. It's got a shipping tag on it, too. Ray tells him it's going to his daughter in Madison. "I'll be damned," Ervin says, laughing, lighting up another cigarette.

THE RECORD PLAYER

On the first anniversary of my father's death, I called my mother. "It's been a year," she said. "The widow support group says I should make some new plans now."

"What do you mean, plans?" I asked.

"First thing I need to do," she said, "is to get rid of his things."

"Things like what?"

"Clothes, shoes, junk. All that stuff that I just don't know why I was keeping around anyway."

I tried to think of what he had left: old 78 records, his locked army trunk, a shoe polishing kit. I didn't think there was that much. I already had the things I really wanted: a framed greeting card he had given his mother, a picture of him, glassy eyed and drinking beer with his army buddies at Johnnie's Vet's Club after the war. I wasn't sure what my mother was planning to throw away and I wasn't sure I wanted any of it, but I didn't want it to be gone, either.

"What else are you throwing away?" I asked.

"Susan, I'm throwing away anything that isn't nailed down."

My sister had not been informed of this purge. A few weeks later, she called me from Chicago, tearful and angry.

"Can you believe," she said, "that Mom threw away Dad's record player?"

"You wanted that?" I asked

"I was supposed to take it," she said. "Once when we were cleaning out the basement, Mom asked him why he just didn't throw it away. But he couldn't. That was when he said to me, 'I'd like to see you take that someday. Don't let your mother throw it away.'"

"You should have told Mom," I said.

"I don't know," my sister said. "She seemed really happy when she told me it was gone."

The next week I planned an overdue trip to Des Moines, mostly to visit my mother, but partly to find out what else she might have thrown away. When I asked her about Dad's record player, she told me that she hadn't exactly thrown it away, but had donated it to Goodwill. I thought there might be a chance we could find it.

Dad's record player was a mahogany console with a heavy felt-covered turntable and a radio. Someone now would call it vintage, but I couldn't see anyone buying it because it hadn't worked for years; the wood was dull and scratched, and it had a deep cigarette burn on the top.

Dad had once told us of how he had bought the record player right after the war, when he was living alone in the Lincoln Hotel in the small town where he managed a café.

The night he bought it, he had had a party. All night he kept telling everyone, "No drinks or ashtrays on my new record player." But later that night Dad himself put a cigarette in an ashtray there, which then fell out and burned the deep line into the wood.

"Damned if I didn't to it myself!" he told us, chuckling, running his finger along the dark flaking scar.

When I arrived in Des Moines I asked my mother if she had

called the Goodwill about the record player.

"Why, yes," she said. "I did."

"And what did they say?"

"Let's see," she said. "Oh, yes. The man said there was no telling where it could be. They rotate things from store to store all over central Iowa. It may even turn up back here. But it may be sold. They don't really keep track, I guess."

"I promised I'd look for it. Will you come with me?"

"I suppose so." She asked, "But why would your sister want that old thing?"

We went from one town to another, stopping at the Goodwills that were on the same circuit as the one in Des Moines. Mom was ready to leave each store as soon as we found the record player wasn't there. But me, I liked lingering over the junk—dusty glassware, warped pans, cracked ashtrays won at state fairs, dresses, coats, and hats from another time.

In Perry we talked to a man who said, yes, he thought he had seen the record player. He sold it to a man who came here from out east, someone who refinishes old stereo consoles, rewires them, and rebuilds the insides with CD players.

"Well, that's that," my mother said.

On the way home we stopped in the town where my father was born. It is a farming community that was so small it could hardly even support one restaurant. I know this because I've heard of the café my father ran there in the forties. After struggling a few years, he abandoned it and moved to Des Moines, where he remet my mother; a few years later they were married.

Though many of the storefronts in the town are now empty, in a little house near the square there is a thriving tearoom called the Cozy Kitchen, run by two farmwives who opened it after their husbands lost their farms. Few people from town go there, but it is always crowded with people from

Des Moines, who come for the homey potpies, casseroles, or kielbasa, and to get a glimpse of the country life that's vanishing around them.

I wanted to stop at the tearoom on our way back to Des Moines. We had to wait ten minutes for a table.

"Imagine that," Mother said. "And your father could hardly keep his place going."

Mom talked about the coming year as we ate apple crisp with warm thick cream.

"This is going to be a better year," she said.

"I hope so, Mom."

"Last year was awful."

"I know."

She looked hard at me. "No, I don't think you do know. How could you?" She looked out the window and continued. "I couldn't stand that house, living there with all his things, waiting for him to come back and use them."

I didn't answer.

"Honey," she said, "you've got to move on. That's what the support group tells me."

Later, she said, "You know, I've always thought that you should never save anything that you wouldn't want the whole world to see. And you should never write anything down that you wouldn't want your whole family to read. Your father, he saved a lot of things in that old army trunk of his that he would never have wanted you girls to see."

"Like?"

"Pictures of him and his army buddies and the girls, drinking in Algiers. And those filthy letters all the boys wrote."

"Did you read any of them?"

"I read one or two, but they were all the same. All about the girls. You know."

No, I didn't know. Many of my friends can remember their parents' thirtieth birthdays. But my parents' lives before I was born were vast. They were thirty-eight when they were married, forty when I was born.

I suppose I didn't really even begin to know who they were until they were fifty; their lives before me went something like this: They both grew up in rural Iowa, Mom on a farm, Dad, the son of a barber in town. At seventeen, Mom moved to the big city, Des Moines, to go to business school and later work as a secretary. Years passed, World War II, and somewhere between 1945 and 1950 on a trip to California, a gypsy fortune-teller told Mom she would marry someone she had known all her life. She had tried to think. "Whitey Maloney—the town bum!" she had guessed, for he was the only bachelor she knew of left in the county. My father was married at the time. Sometime during the years he owned the restaurant he married a young woman named Jenny, who died suddenly a year after they were married. The restaurant failed; my father moved to Des Moines to work in sales.

"You can ask me anything you want about Jenny," my father had said when he thought we were old enough.

"What did she look like?" my sister had asked.

He closed his eyes a moment and then said, "You know, I can't even remember."

I believed him and I never thought much about her until we buried my father next to her in the family plot, where there's a place for my mother on the other side. I remember that day feeling oddly comforted that someone was lying next to Dad, and that after all these years alone, Jenny, whoever she was, had someone lying next to her.

Over coffee, my mother told me what else she had thrown away: clothes, newspaper clippings, pens, business cards, menus from his restaurant, postcards of motels from his days as a salesman.

"He was such a packrat," she said.

"Did you save any pictures of his family?"

"Oh, of course. Now *those* are things I can understand saving."

"Did he have any pictures of Jenny?"

She smiled as if remembering a secret and said, "No, I didn't find any pictures of her."

"Do you remember what she looked like?"

"No," she said. "She was so young. She was twenty when they married. Your father was thirty."

"Did you know her?"

"I knew of her. I was living in Des Moines at the time."

She paused for a while, looking out the window behind me. Then she looked straight at me. "You know," she said, "they say she adored your father. They say no one was ever as crazy about a man as she was about him."

She took out her compact mirror and applied some lipstick—a bright shade I had never seen on her. Then she began talking cheerfully about the plans she was making; perhaps she would move into an apartment. She wanted to do some traveling.

I was sorry we hadn't found the record player. I thought of how the gruff, no-necked men from Goodwill had probably whisked it away like garbage, while my mother clasped her hands together, glad to get one more sad piece out of the house. I could picture some man in some place like Brooklyn, sanding down the finish, erasing the cigarette burn.

But what I could picture most was my father, slender and mustached, he and his buddies having the time of their lives dancing with the young women in his furnished room at the Lincoln Hotel, where threadbare carpets are rolled up, bottles of beer tipped over, Harry James records cracking and popping under the heavy needle. Later, after all the other guests are gone, a young, shy woman looks for her hat, wondering if she should stay or go home, while my father's cigarette burns into the wood.

Winifred Moranville grew up in Des Moines, Iowa, and has lived in New York City, Oxford, England, and Ann Arbor, Michigan. In addition to writing fiction, she works as a writer and editor specializing in food and travel. She currently lives in Des Moines with her husband, the poet David Wolf.